St. Elizabeth's Children's Hospital, London

Dealing with sick kids can be heartbreaking,
funny and uplifting, often all at once!

This series takes a look at a hospital set up
especially to deal with such children,
peeping behind the scenes into almost all the
departments and clinics, exploring the problems,
treatments and cures of various diseases,
while watching the staff fall helplessly in love—
with the kids and with each other.

Enjoy!

D1622496

Josie Metcalfe now lives in Cornwall, England, with her long-suffering husband, four children and two horses. As a child with a father in the army, she was frequently on the move and books became the only friends who could go with her wherever she went. Now that she writes them herself, she is making new friends and hates saying goodbye at the end of a book. But there are always more characters in her head clamoring for attention until she can't wait to tell their stories.

NICE AND EASY
Josie Metcalfe

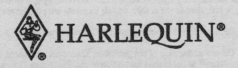

TORONTO • NEW YORK • LONDON
AMSTERDAM • PARIS • SYDNEY • HAMBURG
STOCKHOLM • ATHENS • TOKYO • MILAN • MADRID
PRAGUE • WARSAW • BUDAPEST • AUCKLAND

HARLEQUIN BOOKS
225 Duncan Mill Road, Don Mills,
Ontario, Canada M3B 3K9

ISBN 0-373-63169-3

NICE AND EASY

First North American Publication 2001

Copyright © 2000 by Josie Metcalfe

Visit us at www.eHarlequin.com

Printed in U.S.A.

CHAPTER ONE

Daniel paused suddenly in the entrance to the noisy waiting room and stared at the latest arrival.

She was stunning!

Probably only average height—at least a head shorter than his own six feet—but her slender legs in those jeans seemed to go on for ever. And that wind-tumbled waterfall of blonde hair made him imagine how it would look spread over his pillow for at least the next hundred years.

His thoughts screeched to a halt then rewound for a disbelieving replay.

Him in a long-term relationship? Hardly! He was the perennial bachelor of the accident and emergency department who limited himself to nothing more than flirting and teasing.

Anyway, to find her in the A and E waiting room at Lizzie's meant that she was probably the parent of one of their patients—one of the noisy group playing in the toy area on the other side of the waiting area—and more than likely married.

Why did that thought cause a strange, heavy feeling inside him? It was hardly the first time he'd found a woman attractive and it certainly wouldn't be the last...

Even so, there was something about her that wouldn't easily allow him to drag his eyes away and his body back to work.

He watched for a moment more while her intelligent

grey eyes scanned the cheerful room between them, apparently cataloguing everything from the fully occupied rows of chairs to the group of increasingly exuberant children sharing the play area.

Her eyes moved on along the row of cubicles, glancing at the array of brightly coloured information posters displayed on the walls between each of them as she worked her way towards the doorway where he was leaning.

It would be just seconds before she finally noticed him standing there, and he was just preparing to throw her one of his trade mark dazzling smiles as soon as their eyes met when there was a joyous shout from the other end of the department.

'Annie!'

The word was almost a shriek, but over the sound of several children now fighting over a toy in the play area it hardly registered.

Except on Sarian.

'Maddie!' She was already grinning as she whirled to face the woman hurrying towards her.

She'd been quite happy taking the chance to have a leisurely look round the place she would be starting work in tomorrow, but her friend had obviously caught sight of her. Now, nothing short of an exuberant hug would do.

'You're too early. I don't finish for at least an hour,' Maddie complained as she stepped back and straightened her tabard-style apron, the gleam of laughter in her green-gold eyes belying the words.

'I know. But I wanted to get the journey over before it got dark, and the roads were relatively clear. At this time of year the light seems to go almost as soon as lunch is over, and they were threatening more rain.'

'How much stuff have you brought with you? Did your little Mini scrape the ground all the way here? Do you want the keys so you can start moving things into the flat?'

Sarian held up her hand and counted her fingers off as she answered the questions in order.

'One, everything I own in the world. Two, haven't got it any more. I didn't think I'd need it in central London and, anyway, the parking would be impossible. And three, there's no hurry about going to the flat. I'm happy to wait until you finish your shift.'

She laughed with delight. It wasn't often she saw her perennially serene friend bubbling like this. 'Oh, Maddie, I *am* glad you told me about the job. It'll be great to work together again.'

'Don't thank me. Thank your predecessor for getting pregnant. That's why there was a vacancy in the first place, and then, when her blood pressure started going up...'

Sarian grimaced. They both knew about the dangers of toxaemia in pregnancy and neither of them would have wished it on anyone, let alone a colleague and her vulnerable baby.

'Still, her misfortune is my good luck. I'd almost reached the stage where I would have offered to work for nothing, just to keep myself occupied.'

The understanding expression in Maddie's eyes was enough. Sarian knew she didn't need to say any more about the sad situation she'd needed to get away from.

'You're sure you want to wait around till I've finished?' Maddie asked briskly, obviously deciding that the topic of conversation needed changing. 'I can introduce you to Sister Chappell so you can have permission to have a good look round. I doubt if I'll have time to show you. As you can see, we're pretty busy at the moment.' She gestured with one hand towards the main waiting area where almost every seat was occupied with a patient or family member.

'Excuse me,' said a deep voice behind Sarian, breaking in before she could answer her friend's latest questions. She turned and looked up into a pair of the most amazing green eyes she'd ever seen.

Since she and Maddie had first met at boarding-school she'd always envied her friend her exotic greeny-gold eyes—so much more interesting than her own ordinary grey ones. But these were in a class of their own.

Her heart gave a strange lurch inside her as he held her gaze, only peripherally aware that he was holding a conversation with Maddie at the same time.

'What's the news on young Steve? I presume his blood results came through.'

'Yes. They confirmed the urine test. We managed to get quite a bit of liquid into him while we were waiting for the results but as for getting him to take the charcoal...'

In spite of her inexplicable fascination with the tall, good-looking man standing less than a foot away from her, Sarian was aware that Maddie had turned towards her. It wasn't until her friend started to explain what the two of them were talking about that she was able to force her eyes away from their preoccupation with him.

'He's a young man who got thirsty and decided to help himself to a box of packets of powdered fruit-flavoured flu remedy,' Maddie said.

'Aspirin or paracetamol?' she asked with a grimace, knowing only too well the possible dangers of either.

'Both, in that brand,' said their companion, his deep voice drawing Sarian's attention back to him when she'd only just managed to drag it away.

'Anyway, Tim Robertson was here when the results came back—he's our consultant,' Maddie added in an aside, 'and he decided to admit Steve to the ward for further treatment and observation.'

'I take it you know something about the medical business?' he asked and Sarian found herself hopelessly snared once more by those amazing eyes. It didn't help that they were set in the face of a devil-may-care angel, all lean symmetrical curves and angles, topped by silky-looking old gold hair.

A small corner of her mind was telling her that he was too good to be true. His looks were too perfect, and as for his eyes...their colour couldn't possibly be natural—he must be wearing coloured contact lenses.

And, all the while her mind was rambling, she knew she should be fighting to hang onto her habitual reticence in spite of his dark velvety tones.

'Are you a nurse or just a friend of Maddie's?' he demanded directly, a friendly grin adding extra potency to an already powerful presence. 'I'm sure I haven't seen you here before. I would have remembered.'

'Annie joins us tomorrow morning, taking over from Karin,' Maddie reminded him in a happy rush, barely allowing Sarian time to draw breath. 'She's the one I've been telling you about. We've known each other since we were at school together.'

'So, *you're* the one I come to when I want to find out all Maddie's incriminating secrets,' he said, his smile widening. 'Since she's completely neglected to introduce us properly, we'll have to do it for ourselves. I'm Daniel Burr.'

He held out one lean, long-fingered hand and, quite mesmerised by his larger-than-life presence, Sarian automatically put her own into it.

It felt so big and strong and warm as it wrapped around her much smaller one, but was so infinitely gentle that she could tell he had learned exactly how to control and temper that strength.

'And you are?' he prompted with a twinkle in his clear green eyes and a teasing squeeze of her fingers.

Sarian snatched her hand back, suddenly realising that she'd left it in his grasp for an embarrassingly long time while she gazed up at him yet again.

What on earth was the matter with her? She never behaved like this with *anyone*, especially not a good-looking man like him. It only led to misery.

'Sarian,' she muttered hastily.

'Annie,' Maddie contradicted simultaneously and threw her a startled glance, obviously remembering how reticent her friend had always been about her unusual name. And here she was announcing it to a perfect stranger...

'Aha! A woman of mystery,' Daniel teased with an amused glance between the two of them. 'Just how many names does she answer to?'

Sarian snatched a quick breath as she tried to gather her wits about her.

'My name is Sarian Williams,' she offered quietly, her recently renewed pride in sharing her special name clear in her steady voice and the unconscious tilt of her chin. She hadn't had time to tell Maddie about all the changes in her life in the last few months, but this was one decision she was sticking to right from the start.

'But at school she was usually called Annie,' Maddie added.

'But why?' he demanded. 'Sarian's so unusual. It's a beautiful name, like its owner.'

'I was named after my Welsh grandmother,' she explained quietly, pleased that he'd correctly pronounced it the way she had, to rhyme with Marion. As far as his attempt at flattery went, she'd had many years to learn how to ignore empty words. 'My parents insisted on shortening it to something more ordinary, and it stuck, in spite of the fact that I liked the sense of connection it gave me with her.'

'So, which would you rather *I* called you?' His green eyes were very intent and Sarian had a strange feeling that her answer really mattered to him.

'I...I'll let you choose,' she compromised with a shaky attempt at lightness. 'Most doctors just shout ''Nurse'' without bothering with a name.'

'Not here!' He feigned shock. 'This is Lizzie's, the jewel in the crown of medical excellence. Haven't you heard? We're all one big happy family, here.'

Maddie made a rude noise but he ignored her.

'Have you been allocated a room in the staff accommodation block?' he asked, leaning one shoulder against a full-colour poster depicting common poisonous plants as though settling in for a long chat.

He seemed perfectly relaxed but she had a strong feeling from the intent expression he'd focused on her that there was an unusually keen intelligence camouflaged under all the teasing and smiles. She wouldn't be at all surprised if he was filing all her replies and her reactions in his head for closer examination at a later date.

'Certainly not!' Maddie exclaimed. 'She's moving in with me. We had enough of large-scale communal living at boarding school. We're looking forward to being able to get right away from here when we're off duty.'

'Uh-oh!' Daniel muttered suddenly, straightening away from the wall for all the world as if he were a little boy caught out in some childish prank. 'Here comes Sister Chappell and it looks like she's on the warpath.'

'Sister Brooks,' said the tall austere-looking woman when she came in range, and Sarian remembered her first impression of the woman at her interview. She certainly wasn't the sort of person to allow any slacking in *her* department.

'Sister Chappell,' Daniel interjected smoothly, drawing her attention with a charming smile. 'I believe you've already met our new junior sister, Sarian Williams. Maddie was just introducing us.'

'At some length, apparently,' the older woman retorted wryly, refusing to respond to his cajoling smile as she turned towards Sarian. 'Welcome to St Elizabeth's. I understand you're able to join us earlier than expected. Tomorrow morning at seven-thirty?'

'Yes, Sister.' Sarian's heart sank when she realised that she might have blotted her copybook before she'd even started. She hadn't realised how long the three of them had been talking.

'Uniform all organised, or will you need to do that now?' her superior continued briskly.

'Maddie sorted it out for me,' Sarian explained. 'It'll be quite a change from my last post. We were still wearing pleated frilly hats and dresses with puffed sleeves and Peter Pan collars covered by starched white aprons.'

'Not everyone approves of the change, though,' Sister Chappell pointed out, then gave in unexpectedly to a small smile of her own. 'I must admit, the new trousers definitely make it a lot easier to preserve your modesty when you're dealing with children.'

Sarian returned the smile, suddenly realising that here was another person with a great deal of their personality hidden behind a façade. She had a feeling that her new job was going to be even more interesting than she'd expected.

'Now, then, you two. Time you got back to work. I'll take care of Sarian.' Sister Chappell made a shooing motion with both hands as if Daniel and Maddie were chickens that needed chasing away.

She turned back to Sarian and as she did Maddie signalled frantically behind her superior's back that she would return in half an hour. But it was Daniel who captured Sarian's attention when he kissed his fingers and flamboyantly blew the kiss towards her with a wicked wink of one jewel-bright eye.

'Well, Annie, what do you think?'

Maddie had scarcely let her get inside the door with the last armful of belongings before she whirled to face her.

'It's perfect, Maddie.' Sarian took a look round the tiny living room. It had been immaculately tidy until she'd arrived, but, if she remembered Maddie, it wouldn't take long before she'd found a home for everything. She'd always been a born home-maker and nurturer, right from the first moment they'd met at boarding-school, more than sixteen years ago.

'I was lucky to find it, so close to Lizzie's. The rent's more than one of the flatlets in the staff accommodation and things were a bit tight financially...'

'But it was worth it for the peace and privacy,'

Sarian completed, understanding Maddie's reasoning completely. It dated back to their crowded communal school-days when they'd been looking forward to getting out on their own.

'Not that you'll be getting much of that here,' Maddie added with a frown as she glanced around the cluttered room. 'Are you sure you wouldn't rather have the bedroom? I don't mind having the couch out here. It's got a proper sprung mattress when it's unfolded.'

'I'm not putting you out of your bed,' Sarian declared firmly. 'As long as I can hang a few things up at one end of your wardrobe, I'll be fine.'

'Better than that, I've bought another one with some drawers for your undies and stuff. When are the rest of your things coming?'

'This is the lot,' Sarian said quietly, conscious that pride had once again tilted her chin up by a fraction. There had barely been enough to warrant the taxi they'd used to transport everything here, but the thought of lugging it all in the dark with a steady drizzle soaking everything... 'As I said, I knew that I wasn't going to need a car here and took the chance of getting rid of as much as I could.'

'But, Annie...'

'It's OK, Maddie.' She reached out a hand to squeeze her friend's arm, grateful that her caring nature was as much in evidence as ever. One way and another, Maddie had been worrying about her for as long as they'd known each other.

'I may be travelling light,' she continued softly, 'but I'm also free from financial worries and ready to get on with my life. My only debt is the one I owe you, and I could never repay that.'

'Nonsense,' Maddie scoffed briskly as she shook her

coat off and hung it neatly on the hook behind the door. 'Remember what your grandmother used to tell you. You come from good Welsh stock, and Welsh women have more backbone than ten women of any another nationality. You've achieved it all by yourself. All I provided was the cheering squad.'

'And the listening ear and the shoulder for crying on,' Sarian added, determined to give credit where it was due. Maddie had been her lifeline right from the moment she'd pushed her way through the jeering gang of older girls surrounding the lost and lonely new girl on her first day at boarding-school.

'And a partner in crime for all those pranks you used to dream up,' Maddie reminded her.

'*I* used to dream up? No way. *You* were the one who suggested we set off the fire-alarm at midnight and waited with a camera to take pictures of the nuns when they rushed out in their night-clothes. And how about the time you filled the sugar-bowls with salt? And—'

'All right! All right! Enough!' Maddie laughed. 'But none of that happened before I met you. You corrupted me. I was just a nice little convent schoolgirl till you arrived.'

'Ha!' Sarian was grinning, thoroughly enjoying the fact that they'd slipped seamlessly into their old ways. 'Well, the nuns wouldn't be very pleased with the fact that I've been here for ages and you haven't even of-fered me a cup of tea. Not the way you were taught to treat visitors.'

'Ah, but you're not a visitor, my friend. You're one of the residents, so you get to make your own tea.'

'I suppose I am. Well, how about making it together, this time, so you can show me where you keep every-thing?'

Between the two of them, it didn't take long to brew a pot of tea, and as they sat down Sarian made a silent bet with herself that Maddie wouldn't be able to sit still long enough to drink it.

'I knew it!' she crowed when, just seconds later, her friend was on her feet again, rearranging her bookshelves to make room for the small carrier bag full of paperbacks that Sarian had brought with her.

Maddie stuck her tongue out.

'OK, so I don't like leaving things untidy,' she said defensively. 'It won't take me a minute to put these away.'

'It will be even quicker if we both work at it,' Sarian pointed out as she put her own cup aside. 'The tea's too hot, anyway.'

'It'll be cold by the time we finish,' Maddie warned.

'So you can make me another one,' Sarian said with a cheeky grin, 'while you're deciding what to cook for supper… Agh!'

She shrieked as she fielded the cushion her friend threw at her and lobbed it back.

'This won't get the job done,' she pointed out in mid-volley. 'And it's making a terrible mess of the room.'

'What on earth makes you think I'm such a neat freak?' Maddie demanded. 'I only tidied everything away to impress you.'

'"A leopard doesn't change its spots,"' Sarian quoted. 'You were always the tidiest girl in the school…*and*, talking of spots, you never even had *one* when you hit your teens. Not one!'

'*Some* leopards change, Annie,' Maddie said, her smile fading as she gazed at Sarian over the cushion she'd been using as a shield. 'All you have to do is look in the mirror to see how much *you've* altered.'

'That's just externals,' Sarian muttered dismissively, uncomfortable as ever with the personal turn the conversation had taken. 'I was bound to change from the way I was at eleven.'

She suppressed a shudder as she remembered the tubby misfit she'd been then. It hadn't even improved as she'd got older, the extra height she gained barely keeping pace with the increasing weight the calorie-laden food piled on her. The necessity of braces on her teeth at sixteen had been the final straw for her shaky self-esteem.

'Let's get this mess cleared away so we can have something to eat,' Sarian suggested, eager to change the subject. 'I'll need to try my trousers on to make certain they're the right length. I usually have to take them up a couple of inches or I'm tripping over them. Do you remember when we made a wish that we'd grow at least a foot taller?'

'Thank God we didn't,' Maddie said fervently. 'At least at our height we don't have to go round barefoot so we don't tower over our partners at dances... Ah, that reminds me. There's going to be a Halloween do in a couple of days and everyone's supposed to go in fancy dress. Have you got any prize-winning ideas that won't cost the earth?'

The double glazing at the windows muted the constant sound of traffic but the curtains weren't thick enough to blot out the light from the street lamps as Sarian lay in bed later that night.

The evening had been full of laughter and reminiscences but she'd been aware that every so often Maddie had gone quiet and thoughtful.

It had been as if she was trying to steel herself to ask questions about the events of the last few months, but had then stopped herself in case the wounds were still too raw.

Sarian smiled into the shadowy room. Still the same old Maddie: wanting to take care of people; wanting to take their pain away.

This was a pain that she was going to have to deal with on her own, and she had a feeling that it would probably never completely go away. After all, it was too late now. There was no way to go back and change anything…

She forced her thoughts down more pleasant avenues and felt a smile lift the corners of her mouth at the thought of the job she would be starting in the morning.

Her uniform was pressed and ready. The trousers had needed shortening an extra inch, but that had been quickly done.

Maddie had offered to lend her a large plastic bag to take a spare set of clothes to the hospital in the morning, just in case. You never knew when a quick change was going to be essential, not when you could be dealing with hundreds of different little patients in a day.

Sister Chappell had given her a very thorough introduction to the department, explaining not only the general layout but also taking her through the myriad forms she would need to use to record anything from a patient's case history to requisitioning a fresh batch of sterile supplies or cross-matched blood.

She closed her eyes and reminded herself that she wouldn't be able to work properly if she didn't get any sleep. It wasn't as if she needed to worry about doing the job. She was a junior sister now, and had studied long and hard to pass her exams with flying colours.

It was the icing on the cake that she'd been offered such a plum job at St Elizabeth's. It combined her two great loves—working with children and the high-pressure world of Accident and Emergency.

All the while her brain was busy she was able, more or less, to control her wayward thoughts. That didn't work when she began relaxing towards sleep and her brain was filled with an image of smiling green eyes set between long tawny lashes.

Her heart skipped a beat when she remembered the way the handsome doctor had blown her a kiss and winked at her. No one had ever done that before, so she hadn't realised that it would bring an unexpected warmth to her cheeks and tighten muscles in all sorts of strange and intimate places.

As if he'd meant anything by it, she told herself crossly, thoroughly wide awake again.

She'd met his sort before; there was always at least one in every hospital. The perennial bachelor, full of charm and as busy as a bee as he flew from flower to flower.

He was nothing to worry about. His attention would wane as soon as there was someone new to pursue; someone prettier with a better figure and longer legs. In the meantime...

A little smile curved her mouth as she pictured his handsome face again, and the flattering way he had seemed to concentrate on her when they'd been talking. It had been...pleasant talking to him; pleasant and strange to be the focus of his attention, no matter how briefly.

And he *had* been paying attention to her. Even while he'd been speaking to Maddie he'd been watching her, those amazing green eyes almost a caress as they'd travelled intently over her face before capturing her own eyes.

It was like nothing she had ever known before, this strange tangle of emotions whirling round inside her.

There was attraction, of course, because he was undeniably a very good-looking man, and a frisson of unaccustomed excitement running along her nerves. There was also a healthy dose of trepidation and distrust mixed in, after all, why would a man surrounded by gorgeous women such as her friend Maddie be interested in her?

Still, he did seem to be interested, at least in getting to know her. Whether it was just as a new colleague or as something more personal remained to be seen.

Time would tell, and, now that she had the job at Lizzie's, she was here to stay, so there would be plenty of time.

She turned over in her bed and fussed with the pillow, trying to ignore the way her pulse had speeded up and her breathing grown shallow. And all she was doing was thinking about the possibility that she was finally going to find out what all the books and films were about.

'Don't be a ninny!' she muttered under the duvet. 'You're twenty-seven years of age, for heaven's sake, not seventeen!'

Not that she knew much more now than she had at seventeen… The remembered image of herself at that age rose up in her mind to haunt her…the stones of extra weight, the mouthful of metal and the ghastly home perm that had taken an age to grow out. No wonder she had been so grateful to the gangly youth who had approached her at the school dance—until his friends' laughter and an exchange of money had made her realise that he'd only done it as a dare.

The memory was enough to still the giddy butterflies released by the thought of seeing Daniel the next morning.

Perhaps he was only being friendly. Perhaps he really had felt an initial attraction towards her. Perhaps it was just his customary way with people, the sort of easy friendliness she'd always envied.

Whatever it was, she had to remember to keep her mind on her job. That was what mattered, especially now that, apart from her friend Maddie, she was completely alone in the world.

As long as she remembered not to take a single lighthearted word he said seriously, how could there be any harm in enjoying his company?

CHAPTER TWO

THE accident and emergency department was very warm and bright after the cold wind and early morning darkness outside.

Sarian hurried towards the back of the department to stow her belongings in her locker in the staff room. She'd arrived in plenty of time, but she was eager to meet the rest of her new colleagues.

'Morning, Sarian,' said a deep voice behind her. She whirled and found Daniel leaning against the frame of the door, his folded arms accentuating the width of his chest and his long legs crossed nonchalantly at the ankle.

Her heart gave a giddy skip, totally demolishing her determination to ignore his effect on her.

'Good morning,' she murmured with an attempt at calm as she turned to hang her spare uniform neatly away. She wouldn't allow herself to think about the warm glow of pleasure that had flooded through her when she'd realised which name he'd decided to use. Nor would she allow herself to attach any significance to the fact that he seemed to have been waiting for her to arrive.

For half a second she wished that Maddie were on duty with her this shift, then remembered the zealous look in her friend's eyes and knew that she'd deliberately arranged things this way. She wouldn't be surprised if, by the time she returned to the flat, everything was once again as neat as a new pin.

In the meantime, she was going to have to settle into her new job on her own terms. If that meant learning to deal with this handsome, smiling man, then deal with him she would.

'I'm not late, am I? Doesn't hand-over start in fifteen minutes?' She glanced up at the large clock on the wall and checked the time against her own fob watch.

'Plenty of time,' he said easily, a gleam in those mesmerising green eyes. 'So, how about a coffee? We could continue the conversation we started yesterday. I always feel it's important to get to know your colleagues, their strengths and weaknesses, to help you work with them.'

The fact that he was the first man she'd met that she felt was worth getting to know was enough of a surprise to Sarian. It certainly didn't subdue her hard-learned wariness that someone like Dr Daniel Burr would be interested in her.

She pulled her head out from behind her locker door and stood up, giving the top of her tunic a straightening tug as she abandoned her pretence that there was anything left to arrange in her locker. Finally, she couldn't put off turning to face him properly any more.

'I've always preferred to learn about people from how they *are* rather than what they tell me,' she replied gently, softening the words with a half-smile. 'Are you going off duty now, or might I see you around the department today?'

There was a brief but perceptible pause as a slight frown drew his brows together, and Sarian wondered meanly if it was the first time a woman hadn't leapt at the chance to spend time with him. She wouldn't be surprised. It was a good job he didn't know exactly how tempted she'd been to sit down and gaze into that wicked angel's face and allow herself to be trapped by those eyes...

'You're bound to see me about, one way or another...' he said cryptically, his eyes continuing their thoughtful perusal.

As she walked past him, carefully avoiding touching him as he lounged in the doorway, she wasn't certain whether he'd meant the words as a threat or a promise. She could still feel a prickle of awareness on the back of her neck when she turned the corner out of his sight and approached the nurses' station.

'Hey! Fresh blood!' announced a bubbly blonde staff nurse as she spotted Sarian in her new uniform. 'I'm Jenny Barber and you're a gift from the gods!'

Sarian chuckled. 'That's the nicest welcome I've ever had. I'm An...' She caught herself and deliberately began again. 'I'm Sarian. Sarian Williams.'

'Hi, Sarian. Thank God for someone else with an unusual name,' said the statuesque woman behind the desk, her smile very white against her dark skin. 'I'm just glad we only have our first names on our badges. Can you imagine how long it would be before anyone worked out how to say Charity Ndebele?'

They all laughed and Sarian was more certain than ever that she'd made the right choice in applying for the job at Lizzie's.

Hand-over was relatively straightforward, with few patients waiting for attention and only two waiting for transfer up to wards in the rest of the hospital.

The peace didn't last long.

Sarian was in the treatment room and had hardly finished taping a dressing over a neat superglue job on a gash under a little chin when there was a commotion just inside the big double doors of the foyer.

'Please. Please, help me,' called a distraught voice, the sound carrying clearly over the normal hubbub of the department and silencing every conversation like the slash of a sharp blade. 'Please. Help me. There's something wrong with my baby.'

Sarian took just long enough to hand the parents an explanatory leaflet confirming what she'd told them about the care of their daughter's wound before she took off at a swift ground-covering walk.

'This way,' Sarian called, signalling for the receptionist to page a doctor, quickly, as she beckoned the young woman towards the resuscitation room.

She looked barely old enough to have a child, wild-eyed and distraught and clearly on the point of collapse, but Sarian's attention was drawn instinctively to the baby.

Her eyes took in at a glance the strange blue cast to the tiny infant's face and the way the fragile chest heaved as he fought for every breath. 'Can you tell me what happened? When did this start?'

She was peripherally aware that two men were following them into the brightly lit room but her concentration was all for the struggling child as she lay him on the bed, checked that his airway was clear and rapidly fitted an oxygen mask over his little face.

'He was like this when he was born,' said the young man as he hurried across the room to join them at the child's bedside. 'We thought it was just that he was getting used to breathing after he came out, but it's been an hour, now, and it's just been getting worse and worse.'

'You mean, he's only an hour old?' demanded a deeper and more mature voice behind Sarian and she stepped to one side. Without looking, she knew that it was Daniel behind her and she went to the other side of the bed to allow him more room to approach. 'Which hospital was he born in, to let you take him home in this state?'

'No hospital. We had him at home. We didn't want him to be born surrounded by strangers and pumped full of drugs,' the young man declared belligerently.

'What about a midwife?' Sarian prompted, hard-pressed to keep her tone and expression neutral. 'Surely your doctor arranged for a midwife to be present?'

'I'm not registered with a doctor,' the young woman admitted, her eyes fixed firmly on Daniel as he began his examination, listening intently to the tiny mite's chest. 'And I had to work right up till yesterday, when the pains started, so I didn't have time to go to any antenatal classes or anything.'

'But we both read all the books,' her partner added. 'Everything happened exactly like the books said, but then he wouldn't breathe properly.'

'Is it my fault? Did I do something wrong?' begged the young mother, wringing her hands together. 'Did we miss out on something important in the books?'

Daniel lifted his eyes briefly from his examination of the child and, over the top of his disposable mask, they met Sarian's in a wordless communication across the pitiful scrap.

'I doubt that he's having problems because you did anything wrong, exactly, but—' he began, his tone far calmer that the expression in his eyes had been.

'Then what's the matter with him?' the young man demanded hotly, butting in over Daniel's quieter voice. 'Why can't he breathe properly and why is he that horrible colour?'

'We'll need to do some tests to find out exactly

what's the matter,' Daniel began again as he straightened slightly. He reached out a hand but before he could ask Sarian's gloved hand was already there with a small-bore needle and saline, the port on the giving set ready instantly for any drugs that might be needed.

'What I can tell you,' Daniel continued quietly as he selected a minute vein, hardly bigger than a piece of sewing cotton, and threaded the needle in perfectly at the first attempt, 'is that, for some reason, his lungs and heart don't seem to be coping properly and that is why he's finding life a bit hard.'

'But, why? And what can you do about it?' the young woman demanded, her face quite ashen under the clear fluorescent lights.

Sarian pulled a chair forward and guided her into it, suddenly remembering that it was little more than an hour since she'd given birth to their little patient. A new mother shouldn't really be having to cope with such a situation in this way.

'It could be a reaction to an infection, or his lungs might not be quite ready to begin their work for him, or any one of several other causes,' Daniel explained, his calm voice pitched deliberately in an effort to allay her terror. 'We'll only know what's causing it when we've analysed his blood and had a close look at him. We're giving him oxygen, so his lungs and heart don't have to fight so hard, and fluids, so he doesn't become dehydrated. This will give us a little time to find out what's going on. In the meantime, as a precaution, I'm going to phone for somebody to come down from the cardiac department to have a look at him.'

Their shared expression told Sarian that they hadn't even thought that there might be something wrong with their precious baby's heart.

'Look,' she prompted, drawing their attention, 'I think he's breathing a little easier on the oxygen, and his skin is much pinker now. What name have you given him, or haven't you had time to decide yet?'

While they each took turns to tell Sarian about the process of elimination by which they'd decided to call their baby David, Daniel was sending a blood sample off to the labs with a swab from the child's throat to see if they could rule out any form of infection. Sarian knew that it would be almost impossible for a child to have developed a respiratory infection this severe within an hour of birth, but when she heard that the woman's waters had broken long hours before the child had finally arrived she realised why Daniel was taking the precaution.

By the time the cardiology registrar arrived, still wearing his crumpled blue theatre pyjamas, Ian Fraser was delighted to find that the contacts were already in place around baby David's chest for an ECG trace of the way the tiny heart was working.

As the pulsing neon-green zigzag worked its way across the monitor screen, Sarian didn't need to be a cardiac specialist to see that the trace was far from normal.

'Can you get in touch with my boss, Charles Bruce, and with Tom Farrell up on Intensive Care? It looks as if we're going to need one of his beds in a hurry,' she heard Ian say to Daniel. 'Once we get him settled up there, we can scan the poor little beggar and find out what's really happening in there. I'll get Mr Bruce to look at the results as soon as they're through, but I wouldn't be surprised if it means a quick trip to theatre.'

Sarian's hands and eyes might have been occupied

with filling in their little patient's case notes, but there was nothing wrong with her ears. What she heard made her heart sink. She'd had an awful feeling as soon as she'd seen him that there was something wrong with baby David's heart, but she hadn't wanted to be proved right.

It took less than half an hour for all the arrangements to be made, and by the time the porter was ready to wheel David up to the team waiting for him Daniel had taken the time to sit the young couple down and explain what was going to happen.

Sharron had cried and clung to her partner when she'd heard that their baby was sick enough to need admission to the hospital, and young Jason had looked close to tears too.

Daniel was patience itself, taking time to answer all their questions until they understood.

'Let us know how he gets on,' Sarian prompted as they prepared to follow David. She'd found a wheelchair and suggested that Jason pushed Sharron to give her a rest.

When the young woman was going to have any sort of postnatal examination was anyone's guess, but if the determined look in Daniel's eye was anything to go by it wouldn't be long.

'We will,' Sharron promised over her shoulder as Jason pushed her out into the corridor and turned left towards the bank of lifts at the back of the department. Her eyes were very red in her tear-blotchy face but, as well as a natural trepidation about her baby's health, there was a new air of quiet confidence about her since Daniel's explanations. 'Thanks for all your help, both of you.'

Automatically, Sarian reached for the paper sheet

and stripped it off the bed, the routine calming and familiar as she cleaned the room and readied it for the next emergency.

'Stupid fools,' Daniel muttered fiercely as he came back into the room, the doors swinging shut behind him with a distinctive swish. 'Why do they think doctors insist on going to so much trouble to check up on mothers throughout their pregnancies? Because we haven't got enough to do? Because we're control freaks? Because we want to use them all as guinea pigs?'

Sarian watched in amazement as he strode backwards and forwards across the gleaming marble-effect floor. Was this the same charming, laid-back character Maddie had introduced her to when she'd arrived yesterday? The almost irresistible individual who'd been waiting for her when she'd arrived this morning?

There was nothing easygoing about him now.

'When will they realise that they are risking their babies' lives?' he demanded with a stormy glower, lecturing Sarian now, with fists planted firmly on each hip. 'If that young woman had only taken the time to go to an antenatal clinic, an ultrasound would probably have picked up long ago on the fact that there was going to be a problem, and the hospital could have had everything on hand as soon as he was born.'

Sarian was fascinated to see this new side of Daniel's character. For all his easy ways, he obviously cared deeply about his little charges; deeply enough not to notice when he was preaching to one of the converted.

She tried hard to suppress a smile as he continued to berate thoughtless parents who put their children at risk, but still felt a grin tugging at the corners of her mouth.

'What?' Daniel demanded, suddenly halting in mid-flow. 'I don't see anything amusing in what happened here this morning. That child could have died before they pocketed their prejudices and brought him in. Do you think that's something to smile about?'

'Not at all,' she said, keeping a tenuous hold on her expression. 'What I think is that it's time you had a large sweet cup of coffee. The caffeine and sugar will give you extra stamina and energy to bounce off a few more walls.'

There were several seconds of startled silence as he gazed at her, then he dropped his head back and blew a stream of air up towards the ceiling.

'Lost the plot for a minute, didn't I?' he said wryly and shrugged his shoulders, drawing Sarian's attention briefly to the way his pristine white shirt fitted across the impressive width. 'Sorry for sounding off like that,' he continued. 'It's just...'

'It's just that you care about your patients,' Sarian interrupted gently. 'And I'm the last one to fault you for that, but...perhaps you just needed a reminder that we're both on the same side?'

'Duly noted,' he agreed with a nod, then a wicked smile took over his face. 'Now, did you say something about making me a cup of coffee?'

'Not me,' Sarian said with a laugh as she made for the door. 'All I said was that you might need one. I'm not due for a break for ages yet, so I'm off to my next patient.'

'You're a hard woman, Sarian Williams,' he called after her and she wondered how he managed to give the words such a seductive sound as she made her way back to the nurses' station.

She worked her way through a typical morning's variety of work in a children's accident and emergency department, each different case making her more confident in her new environment.

Previous experience meant she was well accustomed to seeing a variety of broken bones, from little fingers trapped in doors to multiple fractures sustained in car crashes. It didn't matter which hospital she was working in, the children were just as shocked and frightened and her job was just as much about reassurance as it was treating the physical effects of the trauma.

She was annoyed to find that, with each new case, she was half hoping that Daniel would appear, and it took her over an hour to realise, the second time anaesthetist Spiro Kristakis appeared, that he might not even be on duty any more.

She had just detailed one of the juniors to deliver the latest suspected fracture to the X-ray department, a child involved in a fall from a climbing frame in a school playground, when suddenly he was there at the nurses' station.

'I've been looking for you,' he announced boldly, a wickedly knowing gleam in those compelling eyes of his. He was obviously enjoying the effect of his announcement on the other members of staff within hearing and Sarian only wished she were a little better versed in the art of repartee if she was going to try to match wits with him.

'I don't know why. I haven't been lost,' she retorted crisply as she took Mark Greenstreet's name off the board. It was almost time for her lunch break but, as she had a sneaking suspicion that there would be some degree of safety in numbers if she stayed in the department, she turned to collect the next set of case notes.

'Don't you want to know *why* I was looking for you?' he prompted with a hint of pique in his voice.

'I'm sure you'll tell me if it's important,' she replied and looked up at the board to check the number of the cubicle where her next patient was waiting.

'I'm making a special delivery,' he said, moving swiftly to block her passage and holding a small white envelope up between them.

Sarian heard a chuckle behind her from one of the other staff, and felt the back of her neck grow warm. She'd never liked being the centre of attention, not since that dreadful dance when she'd been a plump, ungainly teenager.

'A delivery of what, from whom?' she demanded sharply, her arms wrapped around the clipboard as if she could use it to shield herself from him. 'I'm not expecting anything.'

'You mean she didn't tell you?' The gleam in his eyes grew more pronounced. 'It's your tickets.'

'She? Who? Tickets for what?' Sarian had no idea what he was talking about, but from the murmur behind her the rest of their audience did.

'The Halloween dance,' he said, as if the answer should have been obvious. 'You should just about have time to sort out a costume.'

'Costume?' She was beginning to have a nasty feeling about this, and, from the look on his face, he knew it.

'That's right. You must have seen the posters. There's a big one on the notice-board in the staff room.'

'But…'

'It's a fancy dress do that the staff are holding as a fund-raiser,' explained Jenny Barber, taking pity on her. 'It's a disco held in the physio department gym as a fund-raiser.'

'But…' Sarian repeated, looking from one to the other and feeling almost as if she'd landed in the middle of one of those dreams where no one listened to you.

'And in my hand I have an envelope containing three tickets,' Daniel said, delving in and fanning them out to show her, like a magician at a children's party, 'which I have obtained at great risk to life and limb under direct orders of Junior Sister Maddie Brooks.'

'Maddie,' Sarian groaned as everything became clear. Wait till she saw her friend. She was going to throttle her for this. Maddie, of all people, should know that Sarian didn't go to discos, even fancy dress ones.

'In which case, as I know nothing about it, you'd better *give* them to Maddie,' she managed to say calmly as she sidestepped him and strode briskly towards the cubicle.

Even in the cubicle she wasn't able to escape him. Within minutes he was there, deliberately leaning over her shoulder to take a closer look at a badly bitten tongue.

'You must have been very hungry,' he teased the youngster light-heartedly as he gauged the seriousness of the injury. 'I should ask for a bigger breakfast, next time.'

The noisily miserable young lad was startled into silence by the joking, a feat Sarian hadn't been able to achieve with her own brand of gentle understanding.

'Right, now,' Daniel continued, holding not only the

seven-year-old's attention but the mother's admiring gaze too. 'The bleeding has slowed down, but you've got good strong teeth and they've made a bit of a deep cut in your tongue.'

The child interrupted with a series of gargled sounds, virtually indecipherable as he tried to avoid moving his injured tongue.

'Ah, you speak a foreign language!' Daniel quipped with a grin. 'It just so happens that I am fluent in it, and, no, you won't have to have your tongue cut off!'

The child gave a strangled sound, a cross between a laugh and a cough.

'Ah, you speak in gargle, too! What a linguist!' Daniel continued. 'And you're quite right, you will have to have a couple of tiny stitches put in to help the cut heal more quickly. In fact, I can give you a choice. Do you want me, or Sister Sarian, here, to put them in? I can tell you, she's a dab hand with the embroidery threads.'

He kept up his nonsensical patter throughout the discomfort of irrigating the wound and the series of injections to numb the injured tongue. He even managed to continue without a pause while he concentrated on the beautiful precision of the stitches that would hold the damaged tissues in position while they healed.

'Now, then,' he concluded as he straightened up from his task, 'I got to do the stitches, so, would you like me to get Sister to put a nice big bandage on that for you, or are you quite happy to take it home like that?'

Sarian handed the giggling youngster's mother an information leaflet with a reminder to return in three days but, with the woman's attention fully on Daniel's departing figure, Sarian doubted whether she heard a word.

Not that she could blame her, Sarian admitted silently. He wasn't just a very good doctor with an amazing way with children, he was also the first man who had forced her to see him as a man and acknowledge the fact that she was a woman.

Not that she intended doing anything about it, she reminded herself sharply at intervals when she found herself looking out for him. Even then, she wasn't certain whether she was looking because she wanted to find him or avoid him.

Her vigilance meant that she saw Maddie arrive just before one o'clock to start her late shift, looking thoroughly pleased with herself.

Sarian was determined to find out the reason for her smug look. Was it because she'd managed to finish her self-imposed tidying task back at the flat, or because of her surreptitious arrangements with Daniel about the Halloween disco?

If she was lucky, she should just be able to grab a couple of minutes to grill her friend before they both stepped back into the whirlwind of a busy shift.

She was passing the double doors into the reception foyer, intent on catching up with Maddie and cornering her in the staff room, when she was grabbed by a young pregnant woman.

'Are you one of the nurses?' she demanded urgently, her breathing rapid and her face gleaming with a sheen of sweat in spite of the cold weather outside. 'I'm sorry, I don't know what those new shoulder flash things mean.'

'That's right. My name is Sarian.' Giving her true

name was becoming almost automatic now. 'How can I help you?'

'I'm three weeks off my due date and I'm in labour,' she said, the last few words forced out through gritted teeth as a contraction took hold.

Sarian wrapped a supporting arm around her and braced her while she rode the contraction out, keeping silent to allow her to concentrate on her breathing.

'Wow, that was a big one,' the young woman gasped as it began to ease.

'Here. Sit down before the next one comes,' Sarian advised, grabbing a wheelchair. 'How far apart are they?'

'Thanks,' she groaned as she lowered herself gingerly. 'I was out shopping when they started about an hour ago, at about twenty minutes apart, but then they suddenly jumped to ten minutes so I knew I couldn't get home.'

'You do realise that you've come to the wrong hospital,' Sarian pointed out gently. 'This is St Elizabeth's and it's solely a children's hospital. This is an accident and emergency department but we don't have facilities for maternity cases.'

'I came here *because* it's Lizzie's—' she began, then had to abandon conversation as another contraction slammed into her with the force of a speeding train.

Sarian checked her fob watch. Less than four minutes! This baby was in a hurry!

Crouching beside her, Sarian offered a hand for her to grasp while the young woman fought to remain calm and in control. There would be time to move her to one of the rooms when she wasn't concentrating.

'You said you came here because it was Lizzie's,' she prompted, straightening when the young woman's

expression told her the pain was receding. Sarian
grasped the handles and, in the absence of a delivery
room, wheeled her smartly into the nearest resuscitation room, crossing her fingers that there wouldn't be
a major incident before the baby arrived.

'My baby's got a heart problem. This is where he's
going to need to be as soon as he arrives. It's all in my
case notes but they're at my own hospital.'

Sarian was stunned by the coincidence of two babies
turning up at Lizzie's on the same day, both with heart
problems. At least, with this one, they were having a
few minutes' notice.

She reached for the phone.

Within minutes the room was a hive of industry.
Maddie had arrived and disappeared again in the direction of the sterile stores, convinced that she'd seen
an obstetric kit in there.

In the meantime, Sarian was helping her unexpected
patient to remove her smart yet voluminous navy dress
and maternity underclothes and don a gown while filling in a new set of case notes.

'Well, Sarian, what delights have you conjured up
this time to brighten my day?' Daniel demanded as he
sailed into the room with a wide grin.

It was either the grin or the light-hearted tone in his
voice…or maybe just the man himself, but something
put an answering smile on her face and doubled her
pulse-rate.

Whatever it was, her brain was scrambled for several
seconds before she managed to find a reply.

'Well, Doctor, I thought you might like to play midwife, for a change,' Sarian said with a wink for Wendy
Thompson, now lying on one of the high beds in the
resuscitation room.

'Hey, that's taking paediatrics back a bit further than I usually go,' he quipped without a blink to show his surprise. 'Any special reason why Lizzie's are getting to play stork on this delivery?'

'I'm sorry, Doctor. It's all my fault,' Wendy said apologetically. 'My husband didn't want me to go shopping on my own, but I thought he was just being fussy. I still had three weeks to my due date.'

'Has anyone been able to contact him to let him know what's happening?' This question had to be directed at Sarian as another contraction was robbing Wendy of the wish to waste breath on speech.

She'd automatically reached out for Sarian's hand even though this time she had the support of an Entonox mask to take the edge off her pain.

'Wendy had taken the precaution of carrying a typed sheet with all the relevant numbers…her husband, her doctor, the hospital and the reference number for her case notes. They're all being chased up as we speak. I've also put in a request for one of the ICU humidi-cribs to be brought down as soon as possible. Sister Chappell was going to back that up with a fuller explanation for the relevant specialists.'

'Good.' Daniel smiled his approval and Sarian felt a warm glow deep inside. 'Now all we need is…'

'Got it!' Maddie announced as she elbowed her way in through the big double doors carrying a bulky parcel. 'I knew I'd seen them somewhere. Here you are, Daniel, one sterile obstetric kit.'

'As I was about to say,' Daniel continued, 'all I need now is a sterile obstetric kit, and, before I can say the words, here it is. Do you see how good these nurses are, Mrs Thompson? They anticipate my every need.'

Wendy chuckled weakly. 'I'm getting the strangest

feeling that I've wandered into rehearsals for some sort of medical comedy routine.'

'If you think some producer's going to shout "Bring on the prop," and we're going to hand you a baby we prepared before, I'm afraid you're out of luck,' Daniel warned her over his shoulder as he scrubbed his hands and donned sterile gloves. 'You're going to have to play this scene the hard way.'

'Oh, God, you weren't joking this time. This *is* the hard way,' Wendy declared as another contraction hit, almost before the last one had faded. 'How much longer will it go on like this?'

Maddie had draped the bed and Wendy's legs with sterile towels then set up a precautionary IV line.

'I'll wait till this contraction dies away and then I'll have a look to see how far you've dilated,' Daniel promised.

'I hope it's all the way,' Wendy panted, 'because I really need to push. Now!'

'Not yet, Wendy,' he ordered sharply. 'Let me check that you're ready, first. Put your tongue out and pant like a dog. I promise I'll be quick.'

Sarian found she was holding her breath while Daniel made certain everything was all right. She was nearly as delighted as Wendy when he gave the all clear.

It was some time since Sarian had been anywhere near a birth, and even longer since she'd assisted, so she was amazed that the sense of urgency and excitement that filled the room was so familiar.

It seemed no time at all until the head was crowning, and soon Daniel was supporting a small head covered in a thick thatch of dark hair while he checked to make sure the cord wasn't wrapped around the infant's neck.

'You're doing beautifully, Wendy,' he called. 'That's the worst part over, and, whatever sex it is, it's got a mass of hair. Ready to find out whether it's time to get the ribbons out or a trip to the barber?'

'Come on, baby,' Wendy muttered and drew in another breath.

'It's a girl, Wendy,' he announced as the child slithered into his waiting hands. 'She's a beautiful little girl and that hair is going to look great tied up with a pink ribbon.'

He sounded almost as delighted as if she were his own little daughter and, out of the blue, Sarian suddenly felt the hot prickle of tears threatening.

CHAPTER THREE

'FIVE-MINUTE Apgar score was barely seven,' Maddie murmured as the doors swung closed behind baby Rose Danielle as she was hurried up to the waiting team.

'At least it was better than the four she scored at one minute after birth,' Sarian pointed out, equally careful not to let the new mum overhear them.

Wendy was worried enough about her little daughter without having numbers put on the state of her health. The poor woman had been openly praying as she'd watched Daniel install the tiny blue-tinged body in the oxygen-rich environment of the special crib, tears of mingled relief and worry trickling down her face.

Daniel had refrained from making any wisecracks at that stage, seeming to be quite uncomfortable with Wendy's tearfully fervent state, and Sarian realised that it was the first time she'd seen him at a loss for a quick quip.

It was also the first time she'd seen him blush, when Wendy had insisted on giving her little daughter the feminine version of his name.

Sister Chappell stuck her head round the door just then, with the news that a side room up near Intensive Care had been arranged for Wendy to stay in temporarily, until they worked out what was happening with baby Rose.

Sarian had noticed something during the baby's delivery that she hadn't seen while she was training. Although she didn't want to spend any more time with

Daniel than she needed to, she decided to wait until the two of them were the last ones left in the resuscitation room to ask about her observation.

'Daniel?'

She'd kept herself busy setting the room to rights again while she'd been waiting, but now he'd finished speaking to James Fenwick, the consultant surgeon in whose hands the baby's future now rested.

Her voice seemed very loud in the silence of the room, in spite of the sounds drifting in from the busy department outside the doors.

'Yes?' He turned towards her and hitched one hip on the corner of the bed, then began to swing his foot in lazy arcs that started to mesmerise her. 'Problem, Sarian?'

'Oh, no,' she denied quickly, suddenly wondering if she was about to make a complete fool of herself. But then, if she didn't ask, she wouldn't learn. 'It's just…I was wondering…why did you wait so long before you clamped the cord? I was expecting you to do it as quickly as possible to get little Rose up to Intensive Care, but you seemed to be deliberately waiting for something.'

'I was waiting for the cord to completely stop pulsating to make sure that every last drop of blood drained into the baby's system—it usually takes about thirty seconds,' he explained. 'When you consider that a child that size had little more than an eggcup full of blood in her whole body, even an extra teaspoon could be vital.'

'I hadn't thought of that,' Sarian admitted candidly. 'And that would be especially true for Rose if she ends up having to undergo surgery on her heart.'

'Too true.' He linked his fingers together and extended his arms up over his head in a joint-popping stretch, his shirt pulling tight across his body in a very revealing way. 'Anything else?' he yawned widely and rubbed both palms down his face, the sound of his newly emerging beard clear across the few feet between them.

She was spellbound watching him. It seemed such an intimate thing to see. She could all too easily imagine that it was what he would do in his bedroom at the end of a long hard shift, or when he woke up in the morning after spending the night together.

'N-no. That was all, thanks,' Sarian said, her heart stupidly stuttering right up in the base if her throat.

She hurried out of the room, knowing that her hasty exit had surprised him but thoroughly relieved to find that it was almost time for the end of her shift. She obviously needed a few hours away from Daniel Burr to get her head together, otherwise she was going to be in big trouble.

'Sarian! Hold the door, there's a good girl!'

She stiffened, unable to believe what she was hearing on her own front doorstep. But, when she turned to face the voice, there was her nemesis racing through the rain towards her.

'Thanks! That saved me from having to stand out here getting even wetter,' he exclaimed, then shook his head and shed water like an exuberant puppy. 'How come you aren't as wet as I am?'

Sarian silently indicated the collapsed umbrella dripping in her other hand.

'If you've walked all the way here to give the tickets to Maddie, you've just got very wet for nothing,' she pointed out stiffly, horribly conscious of the way strands of damp hair had escaped and were framing her face in untamed spirals. 'She's on late shift today and won't finish till nine tonight.'

'I know. I caught up with her at Lizzie's just before I came off duty.' He undid the front of his dark brown leather jacket and shrugged his way out of it, then shook some of the water off onto the mat just inside the door. His dark trousers looked even wetter than hers were. At least her padded jacket reached halfway down her thighs and had given her some protection.

'In that case, what are you doing here?' she asked uncomfortably, avoiding looking at him by concentrating on pulling her thick woolly gloves off and tucking them in her pocket, a manoeuvre that required careful juggling of two carrier bags full of hastily grabbed shopping.

She wasn't certain whether there was anyone else in the big old Victorian house or whether it was just the two of them. It was divided into six flats of varying sizes but not all the residents worked at Lizzie's, so they would be unlikely to return until after five.

It wasn't that she was afraid of Daniel, exactly, nor that she thought he couldn't be trusted. It was just that she felt…uneasy around him.

'Where else would I be?' he demanded lightly as he stepped forward to open the inner door that gave access to the two flats on the ground floor and to the staircase that led to the other two floors. 'I live here, too, you know.'

He stepped aside to allow her to walk through and, for the first time, she barely noticed his chivalry nor his wicked grin as she absorbed what he'd said.

No, she *hadn't* known that he lived in the same house, and if she *had* known she certainly wouldn't have been so keen to share the flat with Maggie. She would have found herself somewhere as far from him as...

Oh, what rubbish, she chided herself, calling her spiralling thoughts to order. Of course you would have moved in with Maggie, regardless of who else lived in the house. She's been your friend since you first realised you didn't need an audition to get the part of one of the Ugly Sisters in the Christmas pantomime.

Anyway, this encounter with Daniel was just sheer chance. If she'd been a minute earlier, or he'd been a minute later, they wouldn't even have met.

'Allow me,' he said as she paused at her front door, and before she could sort her unfamiliar keys out he'd inserted one of his in the lock and swung the door open.

'But...' Sarian was almost speechless with shock. What on earth was Daniel doing with a key? 'But, this is *Maddie's* flat!'

'That's right,' he agreed with a cheeky smile but no explanation. He tried to usher her in with a brief touch of his hand at the small of her back and she jumped as if she'd been scalded by the contact, losing her grip on one of her bags of shopping.

'Oops! Here, let me help.' Daniel dumped his damp jacket on the back of a chair, then crouched and began to gather up the apples and oranges now rolling in every direction.

'I can manage,' Sarian insisted, wanting nothing more than to get rid of him before she turned into a gibbering wreck. She stretched out her hand to grab another apple and overreached herself, cannoning into Daniel and sending both of them tumbling into a heap.

'Darling, I didn't know you'd be so eager,' he murmured with laughter in his voice; laughter that she could feel right through her as she lay sprawled across his body. 'Still, that's the story of my life, women throwing themselves at me…'

Sarian froze for several timeless seconds before rolling frantically away and scrambling inelegantly to her feet, her face burning with embarrassment.

'Hey, Sarian.' There was no laughter in his voice now and she couldn't bear to look at him, knowing what she would see. Last time, she'd made the mistake of trying to confront her tormentors, and she'd never forgotten the hurtful glee on their faces when they'd told her the truth.

'I told you, I can manage alone,' she said, deliberately turning her back on him and bending to gather up her shopping again. 'I'll tell Maddie you want to see her when she comes in.'

Her hands were shaking as she picked the fruit up piece by piece, but there was nothing she could do about that when every atom of concentration was focused on listening for the sound of the door closing behind him.

It seemed like hours before he finally moved away but when he pulled the door closed behind him, instead of the relief she'd expected, all she felt was a curious sense of abandonment. It was almost as if the click of the latch wasn't so much shutting Daniel out as shutting her in.

'So, Annie, have you had any ideas about costumes?' Maddie demanded as soon as she came in the door. 'It'll have to be something fairly simple, as well as cheap, because we've only got tomorrow to make them.'

She didn't allow Sarian time to reply as she heeled her shoes off and wriggled her toes in the carpet blissfully before making straight for the kitchen.

'First things first—a cup of tea. I daren't have coffee or I'll never get to sleep in time for an early start tomorrow. Do you want one?'

'No… Yes… Oh, Maddie, for heaven's sake will you stand still long enough for me to talk to you?'

'OK.' Maddie turned to lean back against the cupboard and folded her arms. 'I'm standing still, so what's the matter?'

'Where do I start?' Sarian said and threw her arms up in the air. She'd had hours to stew about the events of the day, and every one that disturbed her sense of equilibrium involved Daniel Burr. Good Lord, if there was one man who lived up to his name…

'Why has Daniel got a key to your flat?' she demanded, as several hours' worth of realisation that the man could just walk in on her whenever he wanted boiled to the surface.

'I've got one to his, too,' Maddie said, clearly unconcerned. 'We exchanged spares when we moved in here, for convenience.'

'Convenience?' Sarian choked as she whirled to face the unmistakable sound of that key being used again.

'Got the kettle on yet, Maddie, my love?' Daniel demanded as he sauntered into view. 'I've brought the biscuits.'

'Kettle's on, now,' Maddie sang out. 'I'm making tea.'

'Tea's fine with me. Here, Sarian, help yourself.' He held out the opened packet and she saw the temptation of thick dark chocolate peeping out at her.

For a moment she was tempted, but then the spectre

of her childhood misery rose up in her mind and she
steeled herself against it.

'No, thanks,' she said, cringing inside at the horribly
prissy sound of her voice.

'Are you sure? By the time Maddie starts planning
Halloween costumes you're going to need all the energy you can get.' His grin was even more of a temptation than the chocolate biscuits he was waving under
her nose. As for the rest of him, he might only be
wearing a pair of jeans and a sweatshirt, but both were
sinfully black and well-fitting, and a perfect foil for his
blond good looks.

'I'll have one. In fact, I'll have a couple,' Maddie
declared. 'And seeing Daniel dressed like that has just
given me a super idea for our costumes, Annie.'

She turned from the work surface carrying a small
tray with three steaming mugs.

'Let's make ourselves comfortable. You don't mind
if we sit on your bed, do you, Annie?'

It was perfectly innocuous question, especially as the
bed in question was still folded away as a settee, but
the idea of sharing it with Daniel had heat creeping up
Sarian's throat and into her cheeks.

It didn't help that Daniel waited until Sarian had
chosen to sit at one end, then sat himself right next to
her when there was plenty of room to spread out, and
even another chair he could have chosen.

She glanced pointedly at the chair and when she noticed that it still had his jacket draped over the back
from their encounter earlier today the heat bloomed in
her cheeks again.

'Tell me about these costumes,' Daniel invited as he
leaned back in the settee and stretched long legs out in
front of him.

'It was the contrast that gave it to me,' Maddie explained with a gesture towards Daniel—a gesture that drew Sarian's eyes back towards him no matter how she fought it. 'You know…dark and light, day and night, good and evil, youth and old age.'

'And?' Sarian was intrigued now. She couldn't see where this was leading. Not that it had anything to do with *her* as she wasn't going to be going to the disco, anyway.

'And, I thought about making a costume that's a long mediaeval gown with one half white and the other in black. And a pointed hat to match. And if we made up our faces so that one side was the pale beautiful princess and the other was the dark ugly old crone…'

'With the two of you made up as mirror images of each other,' Daniel added, obviously grasping the concept immediately. 'It's a great idea, Maddie, and so simple. I never would have thought it.'

'But, I'm not going to—' Sarian began, only to be streamrollered by Maddie.

'And the best part is that no one, apart from the three of us, will have any idea who we are. We'll be completely anonymous.'

Maddie's green-gold eyes were fixed firmly on Sarian's and she felt almost like squirming under their gaze. Her friend knew only too well what had happened at that long-ago dance and knew that ever since then Sarian had fought shy of drawing any attention to herself. But she was obviously determined that her friend was going to go to the Halloween disco with her and had tried to find a way to make the prospect less daunting.

Sarian subsided into silence. There was no way she was going to debate the subject in front of Daniel. She would wait till he'd gone…if he ever went back to his own flat.

'How about you, Danny boy?' Maddie quizzed. 'What are you going to be wearing?'

'Oh, I thought I'd go disguised as a doctor,' he said, straight-faced. 'I might be able to borrow a white coat from someone…'

Maddie blew a raspberry at him as she aimed a small cushion at his head.

Her aim was off, and it was Sarian who nearly felt the impact of the missile. At the last second Daniel reached out and swiped it out of the air, then turned and presented it to Sarian as though it were a priceless gift.

'Wilt thou keep it, my lady, or dost thou want me to return it in the spirit in which it was sent?'

'I think I'll keep it,' she decided, visions of an out-right battle developing in her head.

'And how wilt thou reward thy knight?' he prompted, batting his long tawny-gold lashes outrageously and puckering his lips as if expecting a kiss.

Sarian froze.

Her heart started beating heavily as she tried to decide what to do.

Daniel might only be clowning around, and his lips did look eminently kissable, but fear of ridicule was far stronger than her wish to know what he tasted like and forced her to scramble to her feet.

'Would you like another cup of tea?' she offered hastily into the startled silence.

Sarian stood in the kitchen with her hands over her face listening to Maddie and Daniel talking at the front door and her face burned with mortification all over again.

'If that's all that's on offer,' Daniel had said, apparently taking her panicky retreat in his stride. On second thoughts, he had decided that it was time to return to his own flat and Sarian had bolted for the kitchen to avoid having to meet his eyes again.

What must he be thinking of her?

It wasn't as though his suggestion had been so outrageous, and any other woman would have been able to take it in her stride as the joke he'd intended.

Except Sarian had never been like any other woman and was totally unable to take such things as a joke.

'Right, any ideas what we're going to make these costumes from?' Maddie demanded as soon as she reached the doorway behind Sarian, apparently oblivious to the tension tying her in knots. 'I thought we could either use a couple of sheets and dye one of them black, or buy some inexpensive lining fabric. What do you think?'

'*I* think I don't like being railroaded into going to a disco I didn't want to attend,' Sarian snapped, unfairly taking her misery out on her friend. 'Maddie, you know I don't like going to things like that. Not since…'

'Not since you were a young girl,' Maddie finished for her, her expression an all-too-familiar combination of sympathy and determination. 'Yes, Sarian, I know all about that, but, for heaven's sake, you're a grown woman now. You've become far too adept at emotional shutdown. It's time you broadened your horizons a bit if you want some fulfilment in your life. Going out to a few discos and dancing with a few men would be a good start, and this Halloween one even gives you the option of hiding behind a costume.'

'I don't need a man in my life to be happy,' Sarian pointed out defensively. 'There are plenty of ways to be fulfilled without a man.'

'Of course there are,' Maddie agreed, far too easily. 'But most of them need batteries to work.'

'Maddie!' Sarian exclaimed on a burst of startled laughter. 'You've really shocked me!'

'No, I haven't,' Maddie retorted through her own laughter. 'We've known each other far too long to be shockable.'

By the time Sarian was settled under the covers she'd conceded the battle and the two of them had drawn sketches and made lists of the items they would need to make their costumes.

She still wasn't happy with the idea of going to the dance, but that wasn't what she was thinking about as she lay in the dusky shadows of her temporary bedroom.

She'd been pulling the settee out to make her bed and, reaching for a cushion to put it onto the pile, had paused as she'd remembered the way Daniel's quick reflexes had prevented it from hitting her.

She remembered, too, her embarrassing overreaction as he'd teased her about rewarding him with a kiss.

But it was the image of the expression on his face that stayed in her mind as she stared up in the darkness and waited for sleep to come.

What had it meant?

She couldn't recall ever seeing it on a man's face as he spoke to her.

And as for his eyes...those wonderful dark emerald eyes that seemed so candid and open one minute, and the next reminded her of some wily, wary animal...

Suddenly her train of thought screeched to a halt.

Wary? What on earth had made her think a self-confident extrovert bachelor like Daniel would have a wary expression in his eyes? She must have imagined it. The look in his eyes was always serious and concerned but it could also be full of laughter and wickedness, especially when he was joking with the nurses or one of their young patients.

What on earth did *he* have to be wary about?

It was a mystery to her, and he was still filling her thoughts and her imagination as she drifted off to sleep.

Sarian was a mystery to him, Daniel realised as he sprawled diagonally across the full width of his bed. The duvet was barely pulled up as far as his waist but, in spite of the chill in the air, his concentration was so fierce that he hardly noticed.

One minute she was a cool, calm, professional woman, and the next she was... What was that expression...? As nervous as a long-tailed cat in a room full of rocking-chairs.

At first, he'd wondered if she'd taken his teasing as an insult, then he'd wondered if he was just moving too fast. After all, they'd barely known each other twenty-four hours.

The trouble was, she seemed to be sending out mixed signals.

He'd easily recognised the way her pupils had widened when she'd seen him and knew it was unconscious proof that she'd liked what she'd seen. What he hadn't expected was that such a simple sign of approval should so quickly be totally swamped by what had looked like fear.

No woman as beautiful and gentle and genuinely nice should ever feel that she had reason to be afraid of him.

The trouble was, he didn't know her, and, much as

he would like to get to know her better—purely as a friend, of course—he didn't think he stood much chance if she shied away at every contact.

'I'll have to have a word with Maddie,' he muttered as he turned over to thump his pillow into a comfortable shape, then had to turn back when he found that his natural reaction to thinking about Sarian didn't show any sign of receding.

'Not a cold shower. It's nearly November,' he grumbled, remembering his vow, when he'd finally escaped the spartan home he'd grown up in, that he wasn't ever going to have another cold shower.

Not even for Sarian.

Hopefully, the more he got to know her, working together at Lizzie's, the less impact she would have on him, he speculated grimly. Although, if the last twenty-four hours were anything to go by, it didn't bode well for his peace of mind.

He had known all his life that any sort of close relationship with a woman would be impossible, so there was no point indulging in 'what if' daydreams.

If he was lucky, Sarian would become another in his select group of friends, like Maddie.

He took a deep breath and released it slowly while he tried to centre his thoughts. He'd had many years of practice at switching off to unwelcome images, but somehow it wasn't nearly so easy tonight. Not when the image he was trying to banish was that of Sarian sprawled all over his body on her sitting-room floor, her face haloed by escaping strands of hair and her dove-grey eyes wide and startled as they gazed down into his own.

'Maddie, I really don't want to do this,' Sarian repeated for the thousandth time as the two of them paused by the door of the physiotherapy department's gymnasium.

Not that Maddie was giving her a last chance to get out of attending. She was just extracting their tickets from the little pouch-style evening bag they'd fashioned as part of their costumes.

If she hadn't been feeling so sick with apprehension she might have been able to appreciate how well Maddie's idea had worked. As it was, the fact that she had her friend's 'dark' side towards her seemed only too appropriate in view of the way she had been bullied into attending the disco.

Her only consolation was the fact that, not only was she too new for many of the other members of staff to know her, but the make-up job she and Maddie had concocted made both of them completely unrecognisable.

Once they got inside the heavily draped room, she planned to somehow manage to evade Maggie, and then she'd be able to go home and forget all about it.

'Hey, you two! You look fantastic!'

Sarian groaned aloud, glad that the music pouring out of the doorway shrouded in orange and black hid the sound of her dismay. She refused to turn to face him but there was no way she could mistake the sound of that voice, not after the last few days in his company.

The wretched man was really taking his name seriously and seemed to have been stuck to her side like a burr almost since they'd met.

'Wow, Daniel!' Maddie exclaimed. 'All this time and I didn't realise that you were the devil in disguise!'

How could she resist turning to look at him now?

He'd been very secretive about what he was going to wear and her mind had been trying to conjure up a suitable costume…but she'd never imagined *this*!

His off-duty preference for black jeans and sweat-shirts, sometimes livened up with a brighter shirt, had been taken to the limit with a black cloak lined with scarlet and a half-mask that covered his tell-tale dark blond hair with the addition of a pair of devilish horns.

'Have you got a tail, too?' Maddie demanded. 'Turn round and show me.'

'Madam! Please! I don't show my tail to just any-body!' He wrapped his cloak defensively around him-self. 'I'm not that sort of devil.'

'Eh! *Bellísima!*' crooned a sexily accented voice in Sarian's ear, startling her as her hand was captured and drawn up to a pair of smiling lips surmounted by an extravagantly curling pencilled-on moustache.

The stranger was certainly the epitome of tall, dark and handsome with the most amazing dark eyes. He obviously thought himself utterly irresistible, especially in his black musketeer's outfit with the enormous white ostrich feather curling over his three-cornered hat… Except Sarian found herself totally unmoved by his practised charm and dark good looks, especially with Daniel just inches away, his green eyes strangely dark and intent as he watched the performance.

'You are ravishing!' her would-be lover declared in a swift breath before she tried to imitate the voice Maddie had been practising on the way to Lizzie's to-night.

'Oh! How kind of you to say such lovely things to an old lady,' she quavered in a creaky voice, for the first time turning her head to present him with the other side of her character.

His eyes widened in shock and his face fell so swiftly and so comically that Sarian nearly burst out laughing on the spot. The fake warts and wrinkles had been worth every second that it had taken to concoct them.

'Ah, y-yes,' he stammered, taking a swift, inelegant pace backwards as his eyes darted from side to side around her, as though seeking an avenue of escape. 'Very…very clever costume, yes?' he said with noticeably less enthusiasm than before, and quickly disappeared into the shadows.

'And so the conquests come and go,' Maddie managed to splutter before she hooted with laughter.

When Sarian finally caught her breath she realised that the tight knots in her stomach had completely disappeared, and that one crazy incident set the tone for the evening.

The Halloween decorations were totally over-the-top, the music was loud and, between them, Daniel and Maddie kept her chuckling for hours with their banter and their outrageous tales about everyone in the room.

Unfortunately, all three of them were on early shift the next morning so it wasn't quite midnight when Daniel escorted them to their front door.

'Well, he certainly played it enthusiastically,' Maddie was saying as she continued their running post-mortem on the evening. 'But if Ian Fraser intends playing "Scotland the Brave" again, he's going to have to put in some more practice on his bagpipes.'

'I don't think Kirsty noticed any sour notes,' Daniel pointed out. 'It's certainly the first time I've ever heard a proposal of marriage broadcast over a disco sound system.'

Sarian pictured the kiss that had accompanied the

proposal's acceptance and sighed rather wistfully. She'd never experienced anything like that in her life.

'Tired?' Daniel asked. 'I don't think you sat down once all evening.'

'And whose fault was that?' she countered.

He'd started the evening off dancing with both of them at once, but every time she'd suggested sitting down to allow him to dance with Maddie alone the wretched woman had seemed to disappear.

Still, surrounded by all those unrecognizable people in the spooky lighting of the gym, she'd found the prospect of dancing with the devil far less frightening than she'd feared.

'If you'll excuse me, I'm going to the bathroom,' Maddie announced. 'It's going to take ages to get all this gloop off our faces, and there isn't room for both of us in the bathroom at once.'

She reached up and wrapped her arms around Daniel's neck, giving him a careful hug.

'Thanks for helping to make it a lovely evening, Danny boy,' she said. 'Oops! Don't want to get this muck all over your devil outfit. See you in the morning.'

'Night, Maddie. Sleep well,' Daniel said, his smile not nearly wicked enough for his costume.

He'd taken his horns off so that his hair gleamed pale gold against the black of his clothing, but he was still swathed in the scarlet-lined cloak.

'I'd better say goodnight too,' Sarian said quietly, suddenly wishing she had the nerve to give him a hug too.

The careful way he'd treated her this evening, it was almost as though he knew about that first disastrous dance, but she knew Maddie wouldn't have told him. She'd been sworn to secrecy long ago.

'You can't go without your hug,' he said, startling her when it seemed almost as if he'd read her thoughts. 'In fact, you should have two hugs. One for the old crone, because she looks as if she needs one.'

As he spoke he wrapped one arm around her shoulders and pulled her gently towards him.

A frantic voice inside her head was warning her to resist, but her feet were ignoring it and taking the single step that brought her into contact with him.

'And a second one,' he continued, his voice sounding strangely husky now that she was so close to him, 'for the beautiful princess, because she deserves it.'

Before she knew what he was going to do he angled his head closer and brushed his lips gently over hers.

CHAPTER FOUR

'BONFIRE NIGHT, tonight, as if anyone needs reminding,' Senior Sister Maureen Chappell said as she went through her list of notes. 'As ever, we'll be hoping for the best and preparing for the worst.'

It was almost one p.m. and Sarian and Maddie were just beginning their shift, which wasn't due to end until nine this evening.

'If it's anything like last year, we'll still be here hours later,' Maddie murmured. 'There were dozens of them, and as fast as we dealt with them, more arrived.'

'We've already had three serious firework injuries today,' Maureen Chappell continued, 'and I doubt they'll be the last, so we've got a good stock of water gel ready and the wards are bracing themselves for a surge of admissions.'

She glanced round at the members of her nursing team, a tall, deceptively austere-looking woman who had never hesitated to wrap her arms round a child and give him a cuddle if he needed it.

'Don't forget, the effects of burns are not limited to the site of the injury. I know most of you have been through a Bonfire Night at Lizzie's before, but some things are worth stressing. The principles for treating children with burns are the same as for adults, but because they are so much smaller there *must* be a greater degree of urgency.'

Daniel had been standing quietly to one side of the room but he spoke up now.

61

'Remember, many of these children are brought in by their parents and sometimes their clothes are still smouldering. First priority is to remove any burning garments, then establish an airway and immediately begin administration of one hundred per cent oxygen. Check for the presence of conditions warranting immediate intubation, for example, imminent airway obstruction, signs that there might be burns in the airway or a child with a decreased level of consciousness.'

Sarian was watching him while he ran through the list, and was struck by the intensity of his wish that they should all do their best for his little charges.

What he was saying was only a repeat of the work they had all learned before they'd been able to qualify, but he obviously believed in the value of going over the procedure to make certain there were no mistakes.

'When you've removed any constricting clothing, shoes, et cetera, make a quick estimate of the depth and extent of the burn. For speed, we use the Rule of Palms in this department, basing our calculations on the fact that a child's palm covers an area roughly equivalent to one per cent of his body surface area. Check rapidly for other injuries and then cover the burns with wet sterile dressings followed by a dry dressing. Finally, start an IV.'

'Obviously, unless it's a disastrous evening, you are very unlikely to have to do all this on your own,' Maureen Chappell added. 'But if you keep the logical sequence in mind, then you won't be getting in each other's way or duplicating your efforts.'

It only took a few moments more for the senior sister to detail the status of the few patients already in the department, and then they dispersed to begin work.

Everything was relatively quiet for about an hour

with nothing more than the usual assortment of minor ailments and injuries.

Sarian didn't know what made her pause on her way to the nurses' station and look back towards the big double doors that marked the entrance to the reception area.

She caught sight of a woman hurrying through the doors, almost too impatient to wait for the automatic mechanism to work as she carried a keening child in her arms.

'Lisa, is Daniel free?' Sarian called over her shoulder as she quickened her pace towards them.

'Can I help you?' she began, automatically leading the pair of them towards the row of cubicles.

'She's burnt. It's her hands,' the young woman said in staccato sentences. 'Bloody Bonfire Night,' she swore as Sarian lifted the child out of her arms and bypassed the cubicles to hurry her into the treatment room.

The child had stopped her keening cry and was ominously silent now, her little face pinched and grey as she shivered convulsively, her eyes huge and haunted.

'Is it just her hands?' Sarian demanded as she swiftly checked that none of the clothing was burning.

'Yes…ah, I think so,' the woman mumbled as Sarian reached for a mask and connected it to the hospital's piped oxygen supply.

'Here you are, sweetheart,' she murmured as she positioned it snugly over her mouth and nose. 'What's her name and how old is she?'

'Kylie. Her name's Kylie and she's six.' The woman seemed almost unable to bring herself to look at her child, but Sarian didn't have time to worry about that at the moment. It looked as if Kylie was going into shock.

'What have you got?' Daniel demanded, his deep voice very welcome at that particular moment.

'This is Kylie. She's six and she's got burnt hands.'

Sarian didn't wait for Daniel to make his examination, she was already reaching for a size two laryngoscope and blade ready for him to intubate the child.

'Good. Just in time,' he murmured under his breath as Kylie lost consciousness.

'Oh, my God. Is she dead?' the woman shrieked as he ripped the oxygen mask away from her little face and swiftly slid the straight blade into position at the first attempt.

'No. But she is unconscious because of the shock to her system,' he explained briefly, his hands not faltering in their task.

By the time the oxygen was reconnected, Sarian had stripped the clothing off the child's legs and had an IV ready. She had to cut the clothing off her upper half to avoid interfering with the injuries and the oxygen supply.

'It looks as if only her hands are involved,' Daniel reported to the mother as he covered the injured parts with a sterile layer of water gel. 'But she's got partial and full-thickness burns to the palms of both hands, and that could be very serious.'

'How serious?' the woman asked. 'She will get better, won't she? I mean, the skin will heal over, won't it?'

'We won't know how severe the degree of damage is for several days,' Daniel warned as he checked the level of pain relief the poor child would need and filled in the amount already given on her chart. 'It can sometimes take quite a long time before we find out how much of the structure of the hand has been permanently damaged.'

'Permanently?' The woman sounded shocked. 'But it's only a burn. It's not as if she's had a finger cut off, or anything.'

'No, but a burn from a firework is sometimes called a flash burn. The temperature of the fire is sometimes as high as a thousand degrees, so it actually cooks the skin, muscle, blood vessels and nerves, and kills them.'

'But...'

'If the tissue is dead, there is very little we can do but wait and watch while the less seriously damaged tissue repairs itself,' Daniel finished quietly.

Sarian knew that what he wasn't saying was that little Kylie was in severe danger of having to have several of her fingers amputated, even if her hands could be saved.

The consequences if her hands became infected were unthinkable. A child this size had so little reserves to draw on that it could even threaten her life.

'When can I take her home?'

The question was so unexpected that neither Sarian nor Daniel answered for a moment, their eyes meeting over the top of their little charge.

Had the woman really not grasped the seriousness of her daughter's condition? Or did she not care? She certainly hadn't been in any hurry to console the poor little scrap; had hardly glanced in her direction ever since Sarian had lifted her out of the woman's arms.

'Probably not for several weeks, maybe longer,' Daniel said bluntly, probably trying to bring the situation home. 'As I said, at this stage it's very much a case of watching and waiting, and she's certainly in the best place. There's a small side ward up near the plastic surgery department where they sometimes seem to perform miracles. The staff at St Elizabeth's *are* some of the top in their field.'

Sarian was watching the woman as Daniel spoke to her and something about her reaction began to niggle at the back of her mind.

While he arranged for Kylie to be admitted she continued to sift through the impressions she'd been picking up ever since she'd seen the woman come through the doors.

Daniel had returned to Kylie and was bending down beside her talking softly.

Sarian didn't know whether he realised he was doing it, but one hand was smoothing her hair away from her face while the other was holding onto the safety rail at the side of the bed with a white-knuckled grip.

Suddenly, her thoughts crystallised and it took her only a moment to devise a way to test her theory.

'Do you remember what sort of firework it was, and the make?' she asked out of the blue. 'The police will want to know.'

'The police?' the woman repeated, her eyes widening in horror as her hands tightened convulsively in her lap. 'Why would the police want to know? Accidents happen.'

'They will need to check up to make sure that it wasn't a faulty firework,' Sarian invented quickly. 'They can trace it right back through the suppliers to the batch number at the factory. You kept the package and the remains of the one that burnt Kylie, of course.'

'Well, actually, no,' she hedged, clearly uncomfortable. Her eyes were travelling all around the room rather than meet Sarian's. 'I mean, I...I didn't actually say that it was a firework that burnt her, did I? I mean, it was...it was *because* of the fireworks, see?'

There was a hollow silence in the room, broken only by the rhythmic hissing sound of Kylie's breathing and the bleeping of the cardiac trace on the monitor.

'Actually, no. I don't see,' Daniel said, his voice steely and deathly quiet as he straightened up and turned to face her. 'What do you mean it was *because* of the fireworks?'

'Well, it wouldn't have happened if it hadn't been Bonfire Night,' she burst out defensively. 'None of it. But she kept on and on about it, just like she did last year. About going to one of the big displays—like they have in the park.'

She reached into her pockets and hunted about, finally withdrawing a lighter and a box of cigarettes with shaking hands.

Sarian nearly pointed out that smoking was forbidden anywhere in the hospital and especially where there was oxygen running, but the way the woman was trembling she couldn't even get one out of the packet.

Anyway, Sarian was loath to interrupt her now that she was so rattled. Who knew what she might reveal?

'Do you know how much they charge to get into those things?' she demanded, her voice rising to a petulant shrillness as she continued to try to extract a cigarette from the packet. 'Do you know how much money it costs to stand out in the cold and the wet to watch someone set light to thousands of bloody pounds' worth of coloured stars and smoke?'

'At a guess, about the same price as a packet of cigarettes,' Daniel said flatly as he reached for the phone. 'So tell me, while we're waiting for the police to arrive, what exactly *did* you do to your daughter—

just so you wouldn't have to waste the price of your next packet of cigarettes on making her happy?'

'An iron?' Maddie exclaimed as Sarian told her the sickening story. 'She gave her daughter full-thickness burns with an ordinary domestic iron?'

The three of them had taken advantage of a momentary lull to grab a coffee in the staff room. Daniel had gone straight across to use the internal phone while Sarian and Maddie made the drinks, but it was almost inevitable what the topic of conversation would be

'And then she did it again to the other hand.' Sarian shuddered as she tried to imagine the agony the child had suffered, the coffee slopping perilously close to the top of the mug she was cradling between her own palms. 'It's obscene when you realise that nearly one third of all burns injuries to children are the result of deliberate abuse. It's bad enough when they're injured by accident.'

'She's done it before,' Daniel announced grimly as he put the phone down and joined them. 'Once we knew what we were looking at, we checked the computer records. She took the child to the accident department of one of the teaching hospitals last year around this time, but we also found old cigarette burns on the backs of her legs.'

'So, she was deliberately using Bonfire Night to cover up what she was doing?' Maddie said in disgust. 'If you hadn't spotted it…'

'Poor little Kylie would probably have been taken to another hospital next year, and the next.' Sarian was so angry she felt sick. 'Oh, it makes my blood boil. Hanging's too good for people like that. Children are special. Precious. They should be cared for, not abused.'

'Hey, Sarian, take it easy,' Daniel said as he retrieved his cup of black coffee and perched on the arm of her chair. He rubbed his free hand comfortingly up and down her back and it felt so soothing that she couldn't force herself to move away.

Out of the corner of her eye she could see the way the fabric of his trousers stretched over powerful thighs and, with every breath, she breathed in the smell of soap and shampoo and something far more dangerous.

Almost as if he'd forgotten he was doing it, his hand lazily started to explore the tight muscles in her shoulders and neck, and, while they began to relax, somewhere deep inside her a liquid warmth began to grow.

If she was benefiting from his ministrations, it didn't seem to be doing much for him as she could almost see the tension emanating from him.

'She didn't get to see the fireworks,' he murmured softly, his voice sounding strangely bereft.

'Pardon?' Maddie was too far away to have heard clearly.

'Poor little scrap was telling me that she'd never even got to see the fireworks.'

The three of them were silent for a moment when suddenly Sarian remembered something.

'There's a display outside the front of Lizzie's, isn't there?' She checked her fob watch. 'It starts at seven, doesn't it? Do you think she'd be able to see any of it from upstairs?'

Daniel swooped forward to deposit his mug and wrapped both arms around her in a swift hug, his grin almost blinding.

'I'll ring up straight away and find out where they've

put her. I'm sure someone will be able to find her a window to look out of before they settle her down. Poor kid needs something nice to happen today.'

Sarian sat very still while he made his phone call, trying to get her racing pulse under control again.

It had only been an exuberant hug, for heaven's sake, not a declaration of undying love...

But, platonic as it had been, it had been nice to feel his arms wrapped around her, hauling her against the powerful breadth of his chest.

In fact, now that she thought about it, it hadn't felt in the least bit strange or frightening.

Perhaps that was because she was becoming accustomed to working side by side with him when they were taking care of their patients. Or perhaps it was because she had started relaxing around him, knowing that he was becoming a trustworthy friend.

Whatever the reason, she wouldn't have minded if the hug that had started out so fleeting had lasted long enough for her to savour it.

'Anybody here ready to deal with a tearful child and a dislocated thumb?' Maureen Chappell asked, her head stuck round the edge of the door. 'Maddie, could you take over in triage when you've finished your break?'

'I'll take care of the tears until Daniel's free to do the reduction,' Sarian said and quickly drained the last of her coffee.

She could hear her latest charge all the way from here, sobbing his little heart out.

'Oh, sweetheart, does it hurt lots?' she asked as she worked quickly, wanting to administer Entonox as soon as possible.

'I don't think that's what he's worried about,' his

mother said wryly over the top of the wails as she tried to stop her young son from fighting Sarian.

Once his cries were slightly muffled by the mask she continued. 'We were on our way to a fireworks display when he fell, and now he's going to miss it.'

'Not necessarily,' Sarian said with a wink and bent down close to the child cradled on her lap. 'Hey, Steven, want to know a secret?'

'No,' he sobbed and shook his head. 'I want to s-see the f-firew-works.'

'It's a secret about fireworks,' she promised.

That caught his attention. In the space of a few seconds the volume went from deafening to sniffles.

'What fireworks?' he demanded with a scowl, his speech beginning to slur slightly as the Entonox began to take effect.

Sarian crouched down beside him to whisper in his ear, making as big a drama out of it as possible.

'We're having fireworks *here,*' she said, making sure the child's mother could hear too.

'Here? Inside?' He forced his eyes wide open, obviously muzzy enough from the sedative effect of the gas to doubt what he was hearing.

'No. Outside,' she clarified, explaining for his smiling parent. 'Just round the corner where the two arms of the hospital make an angle.'

'Will I be able to take him to watch?' his mother asked.

'As soon as his thumb's been sorted out,' Sarian promised, her ears picking up the sound of Daniel's feet approaching.

'*What's* happening as soon as his thumb's sorted out?' Daniel demanded as he entered the treatment room. 'Are you hatching secrets in here?'

He introduced himself briefly, then concentrated on examining the misshapen little thumb, all the while pretending that he didn't know what the secret was.

Steven's hand looked so very small and chubby against Daniel's much larger one, and when he gently grasped the little thumb the youngster automatically opened his mouth to object. But by that time an audible click told Sarian the job was done.

'Good lad,' Daniel said as he removed the Entonox mask. 'All fixed.' He straightened and turned to Sarian. 'If you just put some micropore strapping around the thumb, for support,' he directed.

'Fireworks now?' demanded the groggy youngster.

'As soon as I've put a bandage on,' Sarian promised, knowing he needed a little while for the effects of the Entonox to leave him before he would be able to walk without wobbling. 'They won't be starting for a few minutes, so you won't miss anything yet.'

She was just waving young Steven on his way to the firework display when there was the sound of a volley of explosions that signalled the start of the display.

Any member of staff who had a few free minutes made for the nearest window overlooking the scene to catch part of the spectacle, but no one could be spared for long.

Gradually the waiting area began to fill with parents and siblings while the burns victims were hurried through for treatment as swiftly as possible.

For several hours there was hardly time to breathe between patients, but slowly the tide turned as the hour grew late enough for their clientele to be going to bed, the parties over for another year.

Finally, it was the end of her shift. Sarian had just made her way to the staff room and was trying to de-

cide between making a cup of coffee or one of tea
while she waited for Maddie when she heard another
ambulance arriving.

She crossed her fingers superstitiously, hoping it
wasn't yet another child condemned to months and
even years of agony as a result of a happy occasion
gone wrong.

There was the familiar sound of the omni-directional
wheels on the trolley as the patient was rushed in
through the emergency entrance not far from the staff-
room door and then an ominous silence.

Something about the change in the atmosphere
caught her attention and Sarian couldn't help herself
from going out into the corridor to see what was happening.

'Sarian!' Maureen Chappell grabbed her urgently by
the elbow. 'Thank goodness you haven't gone yet.
Daniel asked me to get you. He needs you in Resus
Room Two.' She didn't say anything more than that—
not in the middle of the corridor—but she didn't need
to. The expression on her face and the urgency in her
voice lent wings to Sarian's feet.

She tapped briefly on the door before she pushed it
open, wondering what on earth she would encounter
inside the room.

There were two members of staff in the room mask-
ing her view of the patient, and both Daniel and Staff
Nurse Lisa Chan glanced over their shoulders as she
came in.

Lisa's expression was slightly desperate and, knowing how soft-hearted she was, Sarian guessed that the
pretty doll-like nurse was fighting tears over whatever
she was dealing with.

Daniel's expression was harder to read until she

looked at his eyes and saw the same flat hardness she'd seen when they'd been dealing with little Kylie's burns.

Her heart sank. Not another abused child, please, she prayed.

'Leila, this is Sarian,' Daniel was saying as she approached. 'She and Lisa will help you out of your things. Don't be afraid. We're here to help you, and we'll make sure you're safe.'

He stepped aside and Sarian had her first view of the young girl lying huddled on the bed, her clothes torn and dirty and her hands and knees scraped and bleeding.

In spite of the dark honey colour of her skin Leila looked ashen, her dark eyes wide with terror like an animal caught in a trap.

'An ambulance crew came across Leila about a mile from here and brought her in,' Daniel explained briefly. 'They weren't able to tell us anything other than that they found her slumped on the pavement unable to walk.'

'Hi, Leila,' she said softly and offered her hand as the first contact between them. 'How old are you?' she asked, hoping a neutral question would bridge the dreadful silence. It was obvious from the dried tracks on her face that she'd been crying, but now she just shivered and gave the occasional silent convulsive sob.

'F-fourteen,' she said huskily, then warily allowed Lisa to start undoing the buttons on her torn cardigan.

'Do you live near here?'

Leila nodded silently.

'With your family?'

Another nod.

By this time Sarian and Lisa had undone the waistband of Leila's skirt and, supporting her weight between them, they slid it down her legs.

Lisa's swiftly stifled murmur of dismay was obviously the last straw for Leila and her tears began to flow again.

'It's all right, sweetheart,' Sarian murmured as she immediately pulled a blanket up to hide the torn and bloodied underwear. 'I'll take care of it.'

Daniel had carefully stayed in the background while Leila was being undressed. Now Sarian guessed that he had signalled for Lisa to leave because she silently took herself out of the room.

'Do you want me to phone your family?' he asked, his voice full of compassion for the girl's misery, and when she nodded and whispered the phone number he, too, left the room.

Sarian didn't know whether it was something about her, or about the fact that there were just the two of them left in the room, but suddenly the whole story came pouring out.

About the short walk she'd been taking to join some school friends for the evening, for an outing to a fireworks party. About the group of young lads, some of them old enough to have left school and others who could hardly have been older than eleven.

About her fear as she'd been dragged into a basement storage area, her screams drowned out by the sound of fireworks all around; and then the two hours of pain and degradation as she'd been systematically raped by each of them, not once, but several times.

No wonder she had been unable to walk when the ambulancemen had found her crawling away from the scene.

Sarian wrapped her arms round the sobbing youngster and held her tight, rocking her as if she were just a baby.

She'd heard about the increasing incidence of such gang rapes in inner cities, and had been horrified to learn that the perpetrators seemed to feel absolutely no guilt over what they'd done.

It had never crossed her mind that they might see a victim at Lizzie's—the area of the city around the hospital was a relatively safe one.

The police and Leila's parents arrived almost together, and by the time Daniel had completed his formal examination of her injuries, and photographs had been taken to assist in any future prosecution, Sarian was so shattered she didn't know how she was going to find the energy to walk home.

She'd put her jacket on and covered her hair with a knitted 'tea-cosy' hat against the sleety drizzle that had just started, but had paused just inside the doors, dreading setting off.

'Share a taxi with me,' Daniel said, and she didn't really care whether he meant it as an order or an offer, it was too attractive to refuse.

'Yes, please,' she said fervently, needing his company while her brain was too full of the situation she'd just had to deal with.

He stepped out to the edge of the pavement and hailed a cab, turning to beckon her to join him.

In no time they'd been deposited on their doorstep and this time Daniel had his key ready to let them in out of the increasing rain.

'See you tomorrow?' In her disappointment, it was all she could think of as she stood outside her front door. Their journey home had been totally silent when she'd been hoping that he would say something about their involvement in the aftermath of Leila's harrowing experience.

'Tomorrow,' he echoed, suddenly looking tired and preoccupied. 'I've got a load of washing to do before then or I'll run out of clean shirts.'

In the flat, Maddie had left a message on the board in the kitchen to let Sarian know she, too, was doing some laundry.

Sarian sighed. If she was going to be able to talk to someone about this evening's events it looked as if she was going to have to do some laundry too.

CHAPTER FIVE

'No, Daniel. I can't.'

Maddie's voice reached Sarian on her way down the stairs towards the basement laundry room shared by all the residents.

'Look, Maddie, I know there's *something* wrong and the last thing I want to do is cause a problem through sheer ignorance.'

The sound of Daniel's voice down here with Maddie slowed her steps. She didn't really want to intrude on a private conversation.

'You've already asked me once and the answer hasn't changed since then. If you want to know anything about Sarian, you're going to have to ask *her* to tell you.'

Hearing her own voice stopped her in her tracks. Until that moment, she hadn't realised that they were talking about her.

A soft glow of gratitude filled her when she replayed Maddie's words. She didn't know it, but Sarian had just had proof of her friend's loyalty and she couldn't be more delighted.

What she didn't know was what she had done to make Daniel think there was a problem.

There wasn't, not any more.

All that was in the past—even her parents were gone now. So it really was just the two of them, Maddie and Sarian, as close as sisters again and ready to support each other come what may.

With Maddie's unfailing support, she'd turned her life around. Instead of a hopeless drop-out, she'd reached her twenty-seventh year as a woman with a responsible job in a caring profession. She hadn't allowed the traumas of the past to rule her. Just because she chose not to go out socialising at the drop of a hat...

'Was she raped?' Daniel demanded suddenly.

'No!' Maddie retorted, obviously caught off guard or she would have found some way to sidestep answering. 'Look, Daniel, you're not being fair. Sarian's my friend and—'

'And I want her to be my friend, too,' he cut in. 'Maddie, I like her and I can tell that there's *something*... It's almost as if she won't...can't... Oh!' He made an exasperated sound.

'Why does it matter, Daniel?' Maddie demanded softly, only just loud enough for Sarian to hear her over the sound of the washing machine revving up to spin. 'You've only known her for a little while, and if you only want to be her friend...'

'Because I care, dammit!' he exclaimed, his voice carrying clearly and setting Sarian's heart thumping.

'Well, you'd better be careful not to hurt her. She's had enough,' Maddie warned.

'I'm not going to hurt her. I want to help her; to be there for her...'

His words were loud in the sudden silence as the machine switched off and suddenly Sarian realised that she'd left it too late to retreat without being heard. If they discovered her standing here, halfway down the stairs, they might think she'd been eavesdropping on purpose.

She noisily clumped her way down the rest of them, hoping they would think she'd only just arrived.

'Hello? Maddie?' she called and carried her bundle of washing towards the brighter light in the laundry room. 'I heard voices. Are you having a party down here?'

'No party. Just the two of us trying to set the world to rights,' Maddie said as she turned to take her clothes out of the machine. 'This machine is free now. My load is ready to go in the tumble-drier.'

Sarian concentrated on loading the machine, not certain whether her guilt would be visible on her face. She heard Maddie and Daniel talking behind her but conscientiously didn't listen...this time.

When she straightened up to speak to Maddie, her friend had disappeared.

'Where did she go?'

Daniel was leaning nonchalantly back against the Formica-topped table with his hands curled around the edge at either hip.

'We did a deal. I'll fold her sheets and towels when they finish in the drier, if she'll make me a cup of tea and a sandwich.' He grinned, his eyes following her as she leant back against the washing machine, and she was aware that he was watching her every move.

Suddenly she didn't know what to do with her hands. If she gripped the machine behind her it would look stupid, as if she was mimicking his position against the table. But if she folded her arms, it would pull the concealing bagginess of her sweatshirt tight against her, and he would think she wanted to draw attention to her less than perfect body.

'I wanted Maddie to leave us alone,' he said suddenly, the grin fading from his face.

'W-what? W-why?' The words fragmented when she had to swallow nervously in the middle.

'Because we needed to talk about what happened this evening.'

'Which incident in particular?' she challenged, unaccountably disappointed when the topic was work-related. After what she'd overheard she'd been bracing herself for some sort of personal inquisition.

If he'd asked, she'd been determined to turn the tables on him because, since she'd met him and started working with him, she'd been watching him and there were things *she* wanted to know too.

It was perfectly normal for anyone, especially a doctor, to abhor deliberate cruelty towards children. Except...there had been something very personal in the way he'd bent over to talk to Kylie—as if he really knew how much the poor child needed to know she was safe...that someone cared.

Hot on the heels of that thought came another. He would make a wonderful father. She could just imagine the endless patience he would show with a little one of his own—if he ever stopped playing the field long enough to marry...

The thought of Daniel married sent a sharp pang streaking through her and the fact that it felt strangely like jealousy drew her to her senses. How ridiculous. If Daniel wanted to get married that was none of her business. She should be glad that he wanted to be her friend.

'Let's start with Kylie,' he suggested as he settled himself more comfortably against the edge of the table and stretched his long jeans-clad legs out to cross them at the ankle.

'Have you heard anything new? Is it too soon for

them to tell how much of the damage will be permanent?' she demanded, subconsciously allowing herself to relax for a moment when she knew she wasn't going to have to be defensive. Then the memories of the small child's injured hands rekindled her anger.

'It's early days, yet, but it seems as if the damage wasn't nearly as deep as we first thought...but I don't think it's going to matter much,' he added cryptically.

'Not matter?' Sarian leapt on his words. 'How can you say such a thing? The poor little girl has suffered—'

'Hey! Stop! Let me finish, OK?' He waited for her grudging nod. 'Apparently, she was up on the ward and she was just lying there, not responding to anything or anyone—well, she was sedated against the pain so no one thought much about it. Then a policewoman arrived to inform the staff that her mother had been arrested and she overheard. Suddenly, she demanded to know whether she would have to go back to live with her mother again, and when she was categorically told, no, not under any circumstances, it was as if she'd been given a new lease of life.'

'So, what did you mean when you said about it not mattering? Were you talking about the fact that she doesn't have to worry about her mother hurting her any more?'

'I also think she's a child who's had to grow up very quickly and has developed a great deal of courage and determination. She's got dozens of cigarette-burn scars and her life so far must have been hell, but I wouldn't be at all surprised if she amazed the lot of us by the time she's finished. I think she's going to make the best of it, now she knows the abuse won't happen again.'

Sarian wouldn't be at all surprised to hear that Daniel became a regular visitor to the little scrap if only to cheer her on—in fact she would probably bump into him at her bedside when *she* visited.

'I wonder if Kylie's got any Welsh blood in her?' she murmured and smiled.

Daniel blinked at the apparent change in direction then gave an answering grin.

'Something special, is it?'

'If you only knew,' she replied archly. 'One of the most advanced races in the world, the Welsh. They had a parliament, a system of equal inheritance for male and female children, *and* women had an equal right to vote long before the wretched Normans invaded and imposed their narrow-minded male-dominant laws. According to my grandmother, those Normans set civilisation back over a thousand years, and Welsh women have been fighting back ever since.'

Daniel chuckled, drawing her eyes to his smiling face again, and then she was held by the gleam in his startling green eyes. Would she ever get used to seeing them? Would she ever become accustomed to them so that they didn't cause that strange tightening sensation deep inside, that strange twist of awareness that gradually bloomed into warmth?

Suddenly realising that he was watching her again, she dragged her eyes away from his.

'Was that the only news?' she prompted, desperate for another topic to concentrate on before she embarrassed them both.

'They interviewed Leila,' he said softly and waited for her reaction.

'So soon? Was she ready to go through that?'

'Not only ready, but she insisted on it,' he said with

a touch of something that sounded suspiciously like pride in his voice. 'Apparently, she'd poured the whole story out to a nurse with a funny name, and while that nurse with the funny name was talking to her, and holding her while she cried, she told her a very important thing.'

Sarian felt the heat begin to flood up her throat and into her face when she saw the expression on his face, the approval in his eyes.

'Leila said that this nurse told her to remember that whatever doesn't kill you makes you strong, and she was still alive, so she was going to be strong.'

Sarian blinked but couldn't stop the hot press of tears becoming a steady stream as he continued.

'She told the policewoman that the only way she'd been able to cope with what happened to her was to switch off from what they were doing to her and listen and watch as if it was a horrible programme on television.' He shook his head in amazement. 'Apparently, she was able to give the names of all seven of her attackers and a verbal description of each of them that they hope can be made into artist's impressions.'

Sarian sniffed and tried to wipe her tears away but as fast as she did, they were replaced by more.

'Oh, Daniel, she was so young and she was still a virgin before this happened,' she wailed. 'How will she ever be able to cope with a relationship after that sort of mindless bestiality?'

'Shh, Sarian.' She hadn't seen him move but suddenly he was there beside her with a large handkerchief in his hand and an arm to wrap around her shoulders. 'I'll tell you how she's going to cope. She's going to follow the advice of the nurse with the funny name.'

Sarian didn't know whether to laugh or cry and ended up doing both at once.

Daniel's arms wrapped around her and tightened until their bodies met seamlessly from chest to knee, and then he cradled her head in one hand and guided it to the comfort of his shoulder, turning so that he was the one leant back against the machine.

For a moment fear of her own vulnerability stiffened every sinew but it didn't last long. For the first time Sarian knew what it felt like to be cherished by a compassionate male and suddenly she began to wonder what she'd been missing all these years.

'Hey! You two!' Maddie called from the top of the stairs, startling Sarian into leaping backwards out of Daniel's grasp. 'Food will be ready in two minutes. If you don't come up and get it, I'll eat it myself.'

'You'll only hate yourself when you climb on the scales in the morning,' Daniel taunted.

'No, I won't, I'll hate *you* for letting me do it,' she retorted and let the door swing shut with a bang.

Maddie's load of washing had finished drying and Sarian concentrated on pulling it out one item at a time so she wouldn't have to face Daniel. She should have known that he would see through the ploy.

'Sarian?' He grasped both shoulders in gentle hands, pulled her inexorably upright, then hooked one long finger under chin and forced her to meet his eyes. 'You've got nothing to be embarrassed about, you know. We're friends, and that's what friends do—mop up the tears and dispense hugs when required.'

Sarian swallowed hard and nodded.

'Friends,' she repeated in a slightly wobbly voice. 'Right, I'll remember that. And do they also hold the other end of sheets to make folding quicker and easier?'

'Of course,' he agreed easily. 'That goes without saying.'

They were a little longer than two minutes and when they hurried noisily through the door of the flat Maddie gave them each a searching look, but somehow Sarian didn't care. She had a strange feeling that, not only had she taken a giant step forward in her friendship with Daniel, she'd also started to knock the top row of bricks off the high wall she'd built between her heart and the rest of the world.

'You could do worse—a lot worse,' Maddie said suddenly.

Daniel had left a couple of minutes ago after a supper of omelettes and light-hearted chat, promising to load Sarian's laundry into the drier when his came out.

Soon it would be time for the ritual of pulling the sofa bed out and turning the sitting room into a bedroom for the night, but for the moment the two of them were finishing tidying the kitchen.

They had been talking quietly about nothing in particular when Maddie made her pronouncement.

'What?' Sarian wondered if she'd missed part of the conversation.

'As long as you realise what you're getting into, of course,' Maddie continued blithely. 'He's a good man and a wonderful friend, but I doubt whether he's the best prospect for forever after—too intent on his job.'

Suddenly, Sarian knew what Maddie was talking about and heat scalded her cheeks. It was one thing for her to know that just looking at Daniel had a disastrous effect on her equilibrium, but when her best friend started speculating...

'I don't need you interfering in my love life, Maddie Brooks,' she exclaimed.

'Hah! For me to interfere in it, first you have to *have* one,' she retorted logically. 'When was the last time you went out on a date?'

'I'm still settling into a new job in a new area,' Sarian reminded her. 'It'll take time to get to know people and...'

'Excuses!' Maddie accused. 'I know one of the paramedics asked you out a couple of days ago, that dark-haired one with the dimples, and you nearly gave him frostbite.'

Sarian reflected briefly that a hospital grapevine was good at ferreting out gossip, but Maddie was a bloodhound.

'When I'm ready—' she began, but got no further.

'At this rate you won't be ready until it's too late,' she exclaimed. 'The inscription on your tombstone will read "Returned to maker unopened" and it will be your own fault.'

'I'm not going to leap into bed with a man just so I'm not...' Too late she realised her mistake. She'd forgotten how sneaky Maddie could be, making outrageous statements to throw her off balance then closing in for the kill.

'Hah! I knew it! You *are* still a virgin.'

'So what?' she said defensively. 'I haven't noticed you caught up in any bedroom tango since I've moved in here, either. In fact, you could hardly have invited me to share with you if you were in the middle of a hot relationship. Anyway, virginity is hardly a crime, even *this* far away from the days of the crinoline.'

'It is if you won't even give yourself a chance to find the right man.'

'If Daniel's such a good catch, why aren't *you* going out with him?' Sarian countered, finally voicing the question that had plagued her ever since she'd seen how well the two of them got on.

'Oh, no. I couldn't go out with him,' Maddie said, shaking her head. 'Don't you remember my one absolute rule—never to go out with anyone with smaller waist or hip measurements than my own. You, on the other hand…'

'So, let me get this straight,' Sarian said, cutting off any references to her figure. She would have to hold back on the razor edge of her tongue for the sake of their friendship. 'With one breath you're telling me to find the right man and pushing me at Daniel, and with the next you're telling me that he's not the sort to get too involved with because I'll never mean more to him than his career. Maddie, I think you need to think a little longer about the consequences before you start handing out advice.'

She left Maddie spluttering as she set off to check on her laundry. With any luck, her friend would be in her bedroom and settled down for the night by the time she came back—if she hadn't locked her out.

Daniel crowded against Sarian in the lift and she groaned silently.

If Maddie hadn't given her a solemn promise, she would have sworn that her friend had said something to Daniel about her outrageous suggestion.

For the last couple of days, whenever the two of them had been on duty together, it seemed as if she and Daniel were welded together at the hip—or any other part of their anatomy that touched. And half of the time, like now, with the lift empty but for the two of them, the contact was totally unnecessary.

Except her body didn't think so.

Her traitorous body was growing addicted to the feel of his warm strength pressing close, his hand touching her back as he courteously ushered her through a door, or brushing hers as she passed him an item of equipment or a cup of coffee. He'd even contrived to walk home with her on several occasions, sneakily holding her hand or even putting his arm around hers until she stepped away.

The lift arrived up at the roof and it was time to concentrate on the job in hand. There would be a helicopter arriving any moment with a spinal case on board, and she couldn't afford to let her mind wander to the problem of Daniel's unexpected attentions.

'This is Sally,' the paramedic called over the sound of the helicopter's rotors as the patient was carefully manoeuvred out of the belly of the craft and onto the waiting wheeled trolley.

'She was catapulted over her horse's head and onto her own,' he continued. 'St John's Ambulance were in attendance and made sure she wasn't moved until we arrived to put the neck brace on and get her on a backboard. Diminished responses in the lower extremities, blood pressure and pulse elevated—figures on the case notes—IV with saline and she's on Entonox.'

By this time, they'd loaded their patient into the lift and the doors swished closed.

As Sally's range of vision was limited by the neck brace and backboard, Sarian leant over so that her face would be visible to their patient, leaving Daniel to take care of observations.

'Hi, Sally, my name is Sarian. Can you hear me?' she asked, taking hold of the hand unencumbered by the IV to forge a physical contact with the young girl.

'Where am I?' she murmured without opening her eyes, her face very pale against the cloud of tangled dark hair trapped by the strapping of the backboard.

'You've been brought to St Elizabeth's hospital, commonly known as Lizzie's, and you're in a lift on your way down to the accident department.'

'What happened to me?' she asked and Sarian glanced up at Daniel in concern. It wasn't unknown for people not to remember the actual events leading up to their accident and she hoped her question meant just that, rather than evidence of brain damage.

'Apparently, you had a rather spectacular fall off your horse and landed on your head.'

'No!' She grimaced as she forgot about the restraints and tried to shake her head. 'I know about that. I meant, what's happened to *me*, to my body, my neck and back? Are they broken?'

After the worldwide publicity when *Superman* actor Christopher Reeve broke his neck in a similar accident, her questions were hardly surprising.

'We won't know if you've done any damage until we've had a look at you,' Daniel said quietly as they reached the ground floor and he pressed the button to hold the door open. 'It could be several hours before we've done all the tests.'

At the sound of his voice Sally opened her eyes and strained to see him.

'Are you a doctor?'

'That's right. Daniel Burr.' He took her hand and shook it as if they'd just been introduced at a garden party.

'You will tell me what I've done, won't you? I mean, you promise you'll tell me the truth?'

'Yes, Sally, I promise to tell you the truth, the whole truth and nothing but the truth.' He gave her a grin that, to the watching Sarian, held a slightly grim edge. 'That's the way I was brought up,' he added and gave her hand a little squeeze.

The doors of the resuscitation room were wide open and the rest of the team were there, waiting for their fragile burden.

In no time at all she'd been transferred, backboard and all, off the trolley and onto the bed, and then it was time for work to begin in earnest.

It took just minutes for X-rays of the whole length of her spine to be organised and taken, and for blood samples to be taken for analysis and cross-matching. In the meantime, her clothing had to be cut away and her reflexes tested as part of a complete neurological screening.

The whole team had to chuckle when Sally told them that, when her mother finally reached the hospital, she would probably kill her for ruining her brand new jodhpurs and boots, and as for the pure wool Harris tweed hacking jacket...

'As long as you don't tell her that we shredded them for you,' Sarian said, admiring the girl's spirit that she was able to concentrate on the broader aspects of her misfortune. 'It would be bad enough to know they'd been spoiled without adding our part.'

'Was your horse insured?' Daniel asked.

'Of course, and all my tack,' Sally added. 'You have to these days with all the theft going on. But Jester wasn't hurt in the accident, just me.'

'Perhaps you could put a claim in on your insurance

to replace your clothing,' Daniel suggested just as the radiologist came in with the developed X-ray plates.

'I never thought of that. I'll have to tell Mum,' Sally said, unaware that her audience had turned to watch the plates being flicked into position on the viewbox.

There were several seconds of comparative quiet while the radiologist conferred softly with Daniel, their fingers alternately pointing and then moving on as they scrutinised the series of plates.

Sarian found herself holding her breath while she waited for the verdict.

'Sarian?' Sally's voice sounded very small and frightened. 'What's happening? Why has everything gone quiet?'

Silently, Sarian cursed her loss of concentration. She should have realised that Sally would notice the fact that everyone had suddenly stopped talking.

'You call this quiet?' Sarian joked as she reached for Sally's hand again. 'There's every kind of machine bleeping all around you.'

'But nobody's talking any more,' she said flatly, demonstrating once again that there was very little wrong with her brain.

'I'm sorry, Sally, that was very rude of me,' Daniel apologised, turning swiftly back to her. 'I should have introduced the radiologist when he came in but I was in too much of a hurry to have a look at your pictures.'

The room was still quiet enough for everyone to hear Sally swallow and Sarian felt the convulsive squeeze of her hand that revealed her fear.

'And?' Her voice wasn't nearly so grown-up now that she was waiting for the verdict. 'Have I broken my back? Is that why my reflexes aren't normal in my lower extremities? You see, I'm doing Biology at school—working hard to get good enough grades so I can be a vet—and I know what the proper terms mean and—'

'Sally.' She fell silent when Daniel called her name, and she looked up at him with eyes glassy with the threat of tears when he leant over her. 'You haven't broken your neck and you haven't broken your back,' he said slowly and clearly.

'I haven't? You're sure?' The first tears overflowed and ran into her hair from the corners of her eyes.

'You haven't. We're sure,' he said with a smile and added his hand to Sarian's to give her hand a squeeze. 'Remember? I promised to tell you the truth.'

'And nothing but the truth,' she said on a quivery laugh. 'But, I don't understand. If I haven't broken my back, why aren't my reflexes working properly?'

'That's due to something with a very technical term, called bruising,' he teased. 'We're going to have to keep you in here until everything returns to normal and you might need some sessions with one of the ogres from Physiotherapy…'

'But I'm not going to be paralysed?' she demanded insistently.

'Not this time,' he confirmed, 'and you can largely thank your own good sense for your lucky escape because you were wearing all the right protective gear. If you hadn't, it would probably have been a different story.'

Sally's parents arrived just as they were preparing to transfer her up to the ward.

Daniel was able to greet them with the good news and her mother promptly burst into tears.

'I told you she'd be cross about the clothes,' Sally joked, fighting her own tears again as she gripped her mother's hand very tightly. 'You'd better tell Dad about making a claim on the insurance.'

'If you promise to come and visit us when you're back on your feet again,' Daniel bargained. 'And bring a picture of Jester, too.'

It was almost an anticlimax, then, to have to deal with removing pearls from a precious antique necklace out of a little boy's nose.

'It's all part of the job, I suppose,' Sarian said as she took advantage of a quiet moment to boil the kettle. Of course, Daniel just happened to turn up too, and just happened to be standing almost close enough to be her Siamese twin.

'What is?' He leant across her to pour milk into both cups rather than going around her and grinned wickedly at her when she caught her breath at the brushing contact with his body.

It took several seconds for her to pick up the threads of the conversation.

'The variety. It's what makes the job bearable,' she explained. 'If we were dealing with patients like Sally—'

'And Kylie and Leila,' he added.

'Yes. If every patient was like them, we'd all burn out in a matter of weeks. But, mix them up with antique pearls up a nose, swallowed coins, dislocated thumbs, and it all becomes bearable...sort of.'

'Sort of?' he repeated with a lifted eyebrow.

'I meant that it was bearable for us to deal with, not bearable that children were hurting.'

He nodded, accepting the distinction, then took both their cups across to a small unoccupied settee.

Sarian could have groaned aloud but she wouldn't give him the satisfaction. She could hardly wrestle her

cup out of his hand and sit somewhere else so once
again she was stuck with her own private burr.

'You know, sometimes I regret choosing A and E,'
he said in a thoughtful voice and Sarian held her breath,
startled that he should say such a thing. She didn't
think she could ever remember hearing him talk about
his life and the choices he'd made—in fact he was the
most annoyingly close-mouthed person she'd ever
come across.

'Why?' she ventured, afraid the sound of her voice
would be enough to make him clam up again.

'Because we never get to see the end of the story,'
he said a little sadly. 'It's easy with the beads and the
coins and the simple fractures and lacerations, but it's
the other ones...' He shrugged.

'The Kylies and the Leilas,' Sarian prompted softly.

'Yes. The Kylies and the Leilas and all the other
damaged children we see for just a little while.
Sometimes it seems as if we don't do enough for them
because we can only treat their injuries.'

'But that's what we're here for,' Sarian pointed out.

'Yes, and it's important, but they also need treatment
for the injuries to their spirits.'

'Lizzie's does have counsellors and psychiatrists
who will work with them.'

'But most times they're not here long enough for
that to do any lasting good so it's a bit like putting a
plaster over a scar,' he insisted. 'When they leave here
and go back to their lives, the plaster comes off and
the scar's still there.'

'So what do you think we *should* be doing? Is there
a solution?'

'I don't think Lizzie's, or any other hospital, can do
any more than that,' he admitted. 'I think that what

they need is somewhere outside the hospital milieu where they can have the time to come to terms with what's happened in their lives; where they can find out what changes it has caused inside them and how they can learn to live with it.'

'Some sort of refuge or…or respite before they have to go back to the "real" world again?'

'Exactly!' He turned to her and smiled, one of those rare from-the-heart smiles that hit her like a thunderbolt, and suddenly Sarian realised that she was in danger of falling in love with him.

CHAPTER SIX

'AMBULANCE on its way in.'

She heard those same words at intervals throughout every shift, but they still sent a surge of adrenaline to accompany the dread Sarian always felt.

'She's one of ours already, and has taken a sudden turn for the worse. Resus One is free and ready and I've buzzed Daniel. He's going to get in contact with Neurology,' Maureen Chappell said as she accessed the child's notes. 'She's eighteen months old and was born with a brain tumour. She's on her way up from the Torquay area.'

'Torquay? That's almost the other side of the country!' Sarian exclaimed. 'How long will it take them to arrive?'

The phone rang before Maureen could answer, but the conversation only took seconds.

'Not long, at the rate they're going,' the senior sister said grimly as she put the phone down. 'That was the police. Something's obviously gone wrong. They've just tracked the ambulance going past Heathrow Airport at over a hundred and twenty miles and hour and rising. Traffic control have keyed in an emergency override on all the lights between the end of the motorway and Lizzie's so he won't have to touch his brakes till he gets here.'

Footsteps sounded behind Sarian and she turned to watch Daniel approach.

'I've spoken to Ross McKinnon and told him what's

happening. He's waiting for us to buzz him to come down when she arrives.'

'Sister?' a voice called from the nurses' station. Maureen hurried back to take another call then returned immediately with worry clear on her face.

'That was the paramedic on board. Melissa's developed violent hiccups, she's fighting for breath and she's lost the use of one side of her body. They're afraid she's going to arrest.'

Sarian saw the expression on Daniel's face as he reached for the internal phone to relay the latest information to Ross McKinnon. He hadn't needed to say anything for the rest of them to know how serious the situation was.

It sounded as if Melissa's tumour had regrown with a vengeance, and was now pressing on a vital area of her brain. If something wasn't done to relieve the pressure, fast, she would die.

In the distance there was the familiar sound of an emergency siren swiftly growing closer as Sarian and Maureen Chappell moved towards the emergency entrance.

The electronic eye over the doors spotted them and triggered the smooth retraction of the doors. As they stepped out onto the top of the access ramp a blast of icy November wind flattened their clothing against them and rustled their disposable aprons.

A long white estate car seemed to appear out of nowhere, a green light still flashing on top of the roof as it drew to a halt at the bottom of the ramp

'Is *that* the ambulance?' Sarian could hardly believe her eyes. It looked far more like a top-of-the-range family car, apart from the strobe light and the discreet logo on the front.

'It belongs to a private ambulance service,' Daniel said as the staff raced to slide their patient out. 'Real state-of-the-art stuff inside and a fantastic turn of speed, too,' he continued, almost absent-mindedly, his concentration on his view, through the side window, of the paramedic bending over the tiny child.

Then the trolley was racing up the ramp towards them and there was no time to think of anything but the little girl fighting for her life.

'She was on oxygen by mask when we set off, but her breathing suddenly stopped just before we got to Heathrow Airport. I've had to intubate and then hand pump the bag since then to keep her going.' The paramedic had obviously perfected the knack of being able to do several things at once—give a clear résumé of what was going on, as well as keep up his treatment of his patient while they rushed her towards the resuscitation room.

'Apparently, Melissa started having intermittent bouts of hiccups a while ago and the parents didn't think anything of it. This morning it started getting very much worse so she was having trouble drawing a full breath. They were having a long weekend away from home so they had to take her to the nearest hospital who called us in to get her here as quickly as possible.'

He continued his measured squeeze and release technique without a pause. Even when the tiny body was transferred onto the hospital bed he continued, right up to the moment when he could hand over to the member of hospital staff who took up the rhythm.

It took several minutes to complete her transfer to the hospital equipment when the intermittent positive pressure ventilator took over the work of a human hand in squeezing the oxygen into her unresponsive lungs.

By that time Ross McKinnon had arrived.

'Where are the parents?' he demanded as he bent over Melissa.

'Mother travelled up with us in the car,' the driver said. 'I suggested she should sit tight until we got Melissa up the ramp, then... Ah! Here she is.'

Sarian glanced up and saw a very shaky-looking woman in the doorway of the room, escorted by one of the junior nurses.

'Is...is she still alive?' she whispered, her eyes wide with distress.

'So far, so good,' Ross said reassuringly. 'We're doing blood tests and I've arranged for Melissa to have a CT scan so we can see what we're dealing with, but I'm almost certain that it's going to mean another operation.'

'When?' Tears started to trickle down her ashen cheeks as she watched her little girl begin to disappear under all the tubes and wires. 'My husband won't be here for ages yet. Our car couldn't go as fast as the ambulance so we left him behind somewhere near Heathrow Airport.'

Sarian's heart went out to the poor woman. It must be like living in the middle of a nightmare that never ended.

She couldn't imagine what it must have been like to be told that your precious baby had been born with a brain tumour. And then, after everything they'd been through already, to have the tumour return.

'He should have had a chance to get here by the time we've done our tests, but if we need to go ahead and operate...?' He didn't need to finish the sentence. His meaning was clear.

Sarian saw the young woman swallow hard. 'I'll sign any papers,' she said. 'Just...just do what you can for Melissa...please...'

Maureen Chappell went across to speak to the poor woman and, when she disappeared with her escort, Sarian guessed that they'd been directed to the relative quiet of the interview room just a couple of doors along the corridor.

'I think she's just about stable enough to move now,' Daniel said. 'Obviously, the quicker you can get the CT scan done, the better.'

'Too true,' Ross said, his forehead pleated in a worried frown. 'At a guess, it's a matter of minutes rather than days before I'm going to have to cut that section out of the back of her skull again, and have another go at the tumour. Either that, or we're going to lose her.'

They arranged between them for all the various results to be sent directly to the neurology department, then Ross hurried out of the room to make what preparations he could for Melissa's arrival.

The porter arrived to take charge of transporting their little patient, his bright red hair and thin, stringy frame already very familiar to Sarian.

'Hello, Mick,' she said, glancing across at him as she did her part in transferring the baby's connections to the portable system that would keep her going in transit.

'This one requires your special de-luxe treatment,' Daniel said. 'Melissa needs to go to Neurology by the swiftest, smoothest route possible.'

His cheerful face fell.

'Bad is she, poor scrap?' he said in his unmistakable

Irish accent. 'Don't you worry, Doc. I'll get her there safely.'

Daniel beckoned Sarian to accompany him as he went to the interview room to talk to Melissa's mother.

As soon as the door opened the poor woman leapt out of her seat, nearly overturning the small coffee table in front of her.

The junior nurse who had been detailed to keep her company just managed to grab it in time to stop an accident to the tea tray sitting neglected on the top.

'Is she all right? Is she still alive?' she blurted out as she swayed on her feet. 'You haven't come to tell me she's died, have you?'

'No, we haven't,' Daniel said firmly and guided her back down into her seat before she fell down. 'We've come to tell you that she's on her way up to have a CT scan.'

'And? What will happen then?'

She probably hadn't realised that she'd taken hold of one of Daniel's hands and was gripping it so tightly that her knuckles were white and her nails were digging into his flesh.

He didn't make a murmur, just smiling reassuringly as he laid out the possible options for Melissa.

'It will obviously depend on what the scan tells them about the immediate cause of Melissa's breathing problems. She could go to the neurology ward or she could even go straight to theatre.'

'Oh, God, oh, God,' she murmured frantically, probably not even realising what she was saying as she coped with the emotional overload.

'It was only a few months ago that you were at Lizzie's the last time, wasn't it?' Sarian asked, having

picked up a little of the child's previous medical history
by now.

'It was just five months ago that we took her home
again the last time.' She drew in a shuddering breath.
'Sometimes, she seems to have spent more time here
than she has in her own home.'

'Would you rather wait for her up on the neurology
ward? You'll be closer to her and you probably already
know most of the staff,' Daniel suggested.

Her eyes brightened for a moment and she was ready
to leap out of her seat again, then she subsided. 'I can't.
My husband hasn't arrived yet, and he wouldn't know
where to find me,' she said, clearly torn by her need
to be closer to her little daughter.

'That isn't a problem,' Daniel said, finally managing
to extricate his hand from her grasp. 'We'll leave a
message for him with one of the ladies at the reception
desk. As soon as he arrives, he'll be told where you've
gone.'

Almost as soon as he finished speaking she was up
and out of the door, barely pausing long enough to
hurriedly thank all of them for everything they'd done.

'Can you make certain she turns the right way?'
Sarian prompted. 'She's probably too wound up to
work out how to find the lifts.' The junior nurse hurried
out after her to direct her towards the bank of lifts at
the far end of the department and suddenly the room
grew silent.

Daniel had stood up politely, even though Melissa's
mother had been too overwrought to notice the courtesy. Now he was staring blankly out of the small window, apparently sunk in his thoughts.

'How's your hand? Mangled?' Sarian could see the
livid half-moons marking his skin.

'It's a small enough price to pay when she needed someone to hang onto,' Daniel said as he glanced down at it dismissively, not bothering to do more than flex it a couple of times. 'Poor woman, I hope her husband arrives soon. She's so tightly wound that it would take the slightest thing for her to shatter completely.'

He drew in a deep breath and expelled it forcefully, rubbing both hands over his face with a groan.

'Come on,' he said suddenly, whirling and making for the door. 'My battery needs recharging. I think it's time we had a cup of coffee.'

Sarian followed him out of the room, still musing over this further evidence of his caring attitude. She was beginning to think that his devil-may-care easy-going bachelor persona was nothing more than an elaborate front designed to hide the sensitive man underneath.

The trouble was, if that were true, why did he feel he had to hide his real self? He very rarely spoke about himself and, as far as she could remember, had never spoken about his family or his childhood. Had something happened in his past that had made him put up such impenetrable barriers? And had he been hiding behind them so long that he didn't even realise that he was doing it any more?

As ever, when she was thinking about Daniel Burr, one question only led to another, and, unless he were willing to drop his smiling, teasing façade, she had no way of finding out any of the answers.

One thing she did know was that he wasn't averse to taking his turn at the kettle.

By the time she'd followed him into the staff room he'd already switched it on, had two mugs lined up ready and was investigating cupboards and tins.

'Take the weight off your feet,' he ordered, waving her away when she would have offered to help. 'It'll be ready in a second. I'm just looking to see if there are any biscuits about. Aha!' he exclaimed triumphantly.

Sarian collapsed gratefully onto the nearest seat, only realising when it was too late that she'd forgotten to aim for a chair rather than the settee.

'Look what I found...chocolate biscuits!' he exclaimed gleefully as he hooked a small coffee-table over with one foot and deposited the two mugs. 'Help yourself,' he invited, holding the open packet towards her.

Sarian hesitated. They did look so tempting...

'No, thanks,' she said decisively. It was years since she'd made the decision that she was never going to comfort eat again, and she was sticking to it.

'Suit yourself.' He took two out of the pack together and devoured nearly half of them in a single bite. Two more bites and they were gone, and he was reaching for another.

Sarian couldn't help herself following every movement. The lean elegance of his long-fingered hands, the glimpse of strong white teeth quickly hidden behind blissfully smiling lips, the rhythmic clenching of the muscles in his jaw...

'Go on, just a bite,' he coaxed, his words breaking into her preoccupation as he touched his biscuit to her own lips.

Was it the smell of the chocolate, or the persuasive sound of his deep voice, or the wicked grin lifting the corners of his mouth, or the implied intimacy of sharing his biscuit? Maybe it was a combination of all of them.

Whatever, without another second's thought, she opened her mouth and took a sinfully delicious bite.

'Good?' he questioned in a husky voice as she closed her eyes to concentrate on a long-absent pleasure.

'Mmm.' Her agreement was almost a moan. She'd actually forgotten how good chocolate biscuits could taste. It was almost addictive...

'More?' She felt the crumbly texture brush her lips and almost opened her mouth again.

At the last minute she forced herself to open her eyes instead, shaking her head in denial.

'No more?' He shrugged. 'All the more for me,' and he posted the rest into his own mouth.

While they chatted quietly about the day so far, Sarian cradled her coffee-mug between her palms while she waited for it to cool enough to drink. It took her several minutes to notice that Daniel's eyes kept returning to look at her mouth and she grew silent as she started to become self-conscious.

'You've got biscuit crumbs on your lip,' he said suddenly, and before she could do anything about it he'd leaned towards her and was reaching out one hand to brush them away.

At the touch of his fingertips at the corner of her mouth, time became suspended. All she could feel was the slow, gentle stroke of skin against skin; all she could see was the way the green of his eyes darkened as his pupils dilated with awareness.

It was that clear evidence of his awareness that stopped her from moving away.

There was just a single point of contact between his fingers and her lip but the sudden charge of electricity flowing between them was startling. It was the simple fact that she knew he was just as aware of that current that sent an invisible shiver right to the heart of her.

He snatched his hand away as though fearing a burn and the world started turning again, the usual clamour of sounds filling the department reaching them once more.

Sarian had to swallow before she could find her voice, but there was nothing she could do to slow her heartbeat back to normal, nor take away the sensation of warmth lingering at the corner of her mouth.

'I—I'd better get back to work,' she said huskily as she struggled to get out of her seat without brushing against him. She quickly tipped the contents of her mug down the sink and rinsed it out, carefully averting her eyes from his silent form on the settee. 'See you,' she called hastily as she left the room, suddenly realising that he'd forgotten his usual old-fashioned courtesy of standing when she did and wondering why he hadn't said a word.

For the rest of her shift she was working around him as though they were both made of eggshells, while inside she mourned the loss of the easy familiarity they'd started to build over the last few weeks.

She was heartily glad when her shift came to an end and it was time to go home. Maddie was going to stop off to do some shopping and Sarian was looking forward to just a little time to herself.

Perhaps, with a little bit of concentration, she would be able to work out what had happened in those few seconds that seemed to have changed the way the world looked.

'Maddie? Is that you?' Sarian called from the kitchen when she thought she heard the sound of a key in the lock.

'No, Sarian, it's me,' Daniel said and, although her heart had instantly begun to gallop out of control, she clearly heard the front door close with a distinct click.

She turned to face him as she heard his footsteps come to a halt in the doorway behind her with two conflicting emotions fighting for supremacy.

Half of her was still dismayed at the fact he felt quite at liberty to let himself into her home without so much as a courtesy knock. The other half had hardly been able to stop thinking about the intent expression in his eyes when he'd touched her mouth to brush the biscuit crumbs away.

It had taken over an hour before her more down-to-earth side had reminded her that she'd spent the last ten years or more keeping such men at a distance.

It didn't matter that he was the sexiest man she'd ever met, he was still a man.

'Were you looking for me?' she asked, leaning back against the work surface and tilting her chin up at a combative angle. 'Whatever it is, couldn't it have waited until we saw each other at work?'

'It's about work,' he said shortly, with no sign of the teasing smile he usually wore.

For the first time she allowed herself to look closely at him and recognised the barely visible signs of tension that told her something had upset him in some way.

'What?' she asked as a sudden feeling of dread tightened steely fingers around her heart and lungs.

As he began to speak her knees almost refused to hold her up any more and she had to tighten her hands convulsively around the edge of the work surface behind her.

At least he now knew her well enough not to try to soften bad news with ornate platitudes.

'Melissa died?' Sarian repeated numbly, her voice barely louder than a shocked whisper. 'When? How?'

'About half an hour ago, on the operating table,' he said quietly.

'But...but we got her breathing regulated on the IPPV and she seemed to have stabilised by the time she went up for the CT scan. What went wrong?'

'The tumour was massive—almost twice the size of the spinal cord and situated right at the brain stem at the base of the brain. Ross had decided to operate on her in two sessions. First, as an emergency measure, he wanted to take away enough to relieve the pressure on the vital centres that were interfering with her breathing. Then, after she'd had time to regain her strength, he was going to do a second one to try to remove the rest of the tumour.'

'What went wrong?' she repeated, feeling the burn of hopeless tears. Melissa had been such a beautiful little girl. She hadn't deserved to have all that happen to her.

'By the time Ross got her on the table she'd already lost the use of her limbs on one side of her body and partial use of the other side. She'd already had to be put on the ventilator because her breathing had been compromised, then, when he opened the back of her skull, he found that the tumour had invaded both the top of the spinal cord and the lower part of the brain stem.'

Sarian tried to visualise it, the deadly strands of the tumour growing into Melissa's healthy tissues like the roots of some malignant plant, spreading and taking over until they strangled the life out of her.

'He was using microcautery and the microscalpel to separate the strands out one by one and burn them off,' he continued gently as if she didn't know anything about the process. 'But she ran out of time before he could finish. She went into cardiac arrest and they couldn't get her heart started again.'

'Her heart just couldn't take any more,' Sarian murmured, not even aware that she was crying until he handed her a handkerchief to mop the tears up.

As she looked up at him out of swimming eyes she had a vague thought that she was very glad that he hadn't had to give her the news while they were still at the hospital. Any minute now, she was going to be howling and there was no way she'd have been able to walk through the department with streaming eyes and a red nose.

'Oh, God, sometimes this job gets to me!' she exclaimed. 'It just seems so bloody unfair...'

'Shh! Shh!' he soothed as he reached for her and pulled her into his arms. 'We really can't win all the battles, and it was always going to be a race against the devil to help the poor child. To have something like that already growing inside her when she was born meant that the cards were stacked against her right from the outset.'

'But...but she deserved a m-miracle and so did her parents,' Sarian sobbed. 'When we see so many parents who care so little for their children that they abuse them, why does something like this have to happen to parents who love their baby?'

'So, you're saying that only the children who have

abusive parents should get diseases such as cancer?' he challenged.

Sarian was vaguely aware that there was an unaccustomed edge to his deep voice but, just at the moment, she was too emotionally upset to cope with trying to work out why.

'Of course not,' she exclaimed, horrified. 'The children didn't ask to have abusive parents, and they certainly don't need to go through cancer as well.'

'So, who *would* you nominate to suffer from cancer, then?' he asked wryly. 'You've ruled out the children with loving parents because they don't deserve it, and you've also ruled out the children of abusive parents because they've got enough to cope with already.'

'In an ideal world, *nobody* should get it,' she said fiercely, dashing away the last of her rapidly waning tears. She was vaguely aware that he must be using their discussion to try to take her mind off her sorrow but it couldn't dispel it entirely.

'So, we're back to the luck of the draw, again,' he pointed out quietly as he smoothed away a stray tear with a gentle finger. 'Some you win, some you lose.'

Sarian drew in a deep breath, the last of her tears giving it a slight hitch in the middle. Her head felt so heavy that all she wanted to do was rest it against his shoulder and let all her problems take care of themselves. It just felt so good standing here with his arms wrapped around her, and his shoulder felt just right, too. Just tall enough, just broad enough, just warm enough…just right…

'Hey, Sarian, you're not going to go to sleep on me, are you?' he demanded softly, stroking gentle fingers down the side of her face.

'Hmm?' She turned her head to look up at him and

found his face far closer than she expected. *That* certainly chased the comfortable drowsiness away in a hurry.

He'd curved his body protectively around hers and, in spite of her normal restraint, she'd given herself completely into his care as she'd leant against him.

His arm was wrapped firmly around her, virtually supporting her so that she didn't slide down to land in a heap at his feet. His face was close enough for her to be able to distinguish each tawny hair where it was emerging through his slightly olive skin into the faint beginnings of a beard.

She could see each individual eyelash as they framed those startlingly green eyes and realised that each dark tawny hair was tipped with gold.

As she watched, his eyes widened and darkened as the pupils began to dilate.

The message was subliminal but her body recognised it instantly, her breathing becoming ragged and her heartbeat growing faster.

As if in slow motion she watched as he lowered his head to bring his lips to hers in the briefest of brushes, then lifted it again.

He looked down into her upturned face, his expression telling her that he was every bit as shaken as she was.

She smiled.

'Oh, hell,' he said softly, then he kissed her again.

CHAPTER SEVEN

'HE WAS only comforting me,' Sarian reminded herself sternly for the umpteenth time.

It had been relatively dry when she'd set off this morning, although bitterly cold, and she'd had to walk briskly to stay warm.

Now she was approaching the large sign announcing St Elizabeth's Accident and Emergency Department and the squadron of butterflies performing aerial acrobatics inside her refused to go away.

Her hands had been cold in spite of her thick gloves, but now they were sweating at the prospect of seeing Daniel.

She still couldn't work out what had happened between them last night. It was easy enough to put that first fleeting kiss down to his need to comfort her, but the second one...

She was still lost in her thoughts when one of the staff nurses called out a greeting.

'Morning,' she called back, automatically glancing across to reinforce the greeting with a smile...and found Daniel's clear green eyes watching her inscrutably.

She swallowed and dragged in a swift breath, forcing herself to widen the smile to include him.

'Morning, Daniel. It's got colder, hasn't it?' she managed to say as though she hadn't a care in the world, her feet carrying her automatically towards the staff room.

Her effort seemed to have been worthwhile because it was as if her pretended insouciance had broken the ice between them.

The last thing she'd wanted was for their momentary lapse to ruin their good working relationship. And as for their friendship outside work... She valued it too much to have anything blight it at such an early stage.

It had taken hours of thought, but somewhere around midnight she'd realised that his simple kiss wouldn't have ignited the way it had if she'd had her feelings under control. He'd offered comfort out of friendship but she'd reacted like tinder to a match.

It wasn't Daniel's fault that she'd been unable to hold to her decision to maintain her emotional barricades.

All she could do now was make sure that she didn't let him know that it had happened...

Except it wasn't an easy thing to do, not when just the sight of him pulling faces at a miserable youngster in an attempt at cheering him up could tug at her heartstrings. Not when the quick smile he threw her way in thanks for passing just the right piece of equipment at the right time was enough to affect both her pulse and her heart-rate.

And the memories of how sweetly seductive his gentle lips had felt on hers drew her eyes to those lips with the unerring accuracy of guided missiles.

'Sarian?' The concern in his voice drew her out of her crazy introspection and she suddenly wondered just how long she'd been gazing at him this time. Had it been his eyes this time or his lips? 'You're not going down with flu, are you?'

'No.' She might be going down with a bad case of infatuation, at the least, but not flu. 'I'm fine. Really.'

She glanced down at the beautiful neat job he'd just finished. A gash almost the full length of an adventurous five-year-old boy's arm had needed a complete row of stitches to repair the injury done by a stray nail.

'Ready for a dressing?' she asked with a smile.

'Yes, please,' he said, but she could see that, in spite of her smile, he had doubts about her reassurances. Unfortunately, that meant that he would probably insist on quizzing her further before the day was over. 'Ah…and if you find one of your special leaflets for Mrs Jones and…and make sure Luke has an appointment to have those removed?'

She smiled at her little patient as she hid his wound away under a layer of protection, chatting softly all the while. No one could see the inner smile that was a balm to her jangled spirits. It had been a small consolation to her that Daniel seemed to be rather distracted, too, especially when she smiled at him like that.

All trace of distraction vanished when their next little patient arrived, rushed in by ambulance.

'Five-month-old male, Mike Jordan. Looks like bronchiolitis,' reported the paramedic, hurrying straight through to the resuscitation room with the little boy in his arms. 'Fever, rapid respiration, rattles on breathing out, cyanotic, badly dehydrated. He'd been snuffly for a couple of days with a funny dry cough but suddenly started going downhill. By the time we got there he was in circulatory collapse. Couldn't find a vein anywhere so we did an intraosseous infusion. Originally, he was doing well on bag and mask, but just a few moments ago his breathing deteriorated but there wasn't time to intubate.'

'Well done,' Daniel murmured as he quickly assessed little Mike's condition, taking care not to disturb the IV line attached to the needle protruding out of the front of his little leg a couple of inches below his knee. 'I think you've saved his bacon but we need to get moving. If he has to keep fighting for breath like this his heart won't stand it. We need to ventilate, then get some more fluids into him as fast as possible. I'm hoping he'll respond well enough to the intraosseous infusion so we won't have to resort to a venous cutdown.'

While he was speaking he turned towards Sarian who was already reaching for the ready-prepared equipment, the two of them meshing together to work like parts of a well-oiled machine.

Although the optimum angle for lying Mike down was forty-five degrees, until he was properly ventilated the correct angle wasn't going to do him much good.

They were working with almost the smallest size of equipment as Daniel coaxed the laryngoscope into position in his rapidly swelling throat and followed it with an uncuffed endotracheal tube.

Slowly the oxygen-starved blue tinge to his skin receded, replaced by a far more healthy pink, but it wasn't until Daniel finally managed to get a transcutaneous IV up and running, miraculously finding a vein in the back of Mike's chubby little hand, that they all drew in a relieved breath.

As soon as he had a spare minute, Daniel phoned up to Intensive Care to warn them what was on the way up. It would just be a little while before he was certain that little Master Jordan had stabilised enough to make the journey.

It seemed only a few frantic minutes since the child had arrived but when Sarian glanced up at the boldfaced clock on the wall she discovered it had been over an hour.

Daniel stretched and groaned as he rotated his shoulders. Sarian heard the various creaks and pops as the muscles and ligaments, hunched too long over his tiny patient, returned to normal.

'Well, as long as he doesn't go down with an infection, he should soon be good as new after his lungs have had a couple of days' rest,' he said with quiet pleasure.

'Score one for the good guys?' Sarian asked, half afraid to hope for a happy outcome after the defeat yesterday. She'd believed that Melissa was going to win the fight too.

'Hey, chin up. Where's that smile?' he demanded softly. 'There's no point punishing yourself for the ones you couldn't help. Far better to celebrate the ones you can.'

He started to run one teasing finger down her nose but the unexpected contact made her snap her head up suddenly and it ended up on her lips.

There was a breathless pause as her eyes met his and she saw the intense green deepen before her gaze fell to his mouth.

'Oh, hell,' he whispered and she watched his mouth form the words. He began to lean towards her and she half expected him to kiss her again but suddenly he jerked his finger away and stepped back.

He might have broken his physical contact with her but his eyes were still fixed on her.

'What time do you finish?' he demanded suddenly.

'Nine,' she said, her voice sounding hopelessly breathless.

'I'll take you for a meal. Or a drink?' he added as if he'd only just realised how autocratic he sounded.

The defences Sarian had spent years perfecting slotted automatically into place.

'I don't really have the time or the energy to go out socialising at the end of an eight-hour shift,' she said apologetically. 'But thank you for asking.'

The words echoed around the room and inside her head, and for the first time she really heard what she was saying.

It sounded exactly the sort of thing an elderly, repressed spinster would say to the local roué. She waited for Daniel to throw her one of those wicked grins and tease her into changing her mind...only it didn't happen.

Her heart sank when she realised she had probably just thrown away her only chance of spending some time alone with him.

She knew that he had shadows in his past, as she had, and she knew that there could be no future in a relationship between them, but it would have been nice to have the chance to pretend...just for a little while.

'OK,' he said easily with a nonchalant shrug of his shoulders. 'I'll see you, then.'

With a scant wave he turned away from her and strode back out into the department.

'You idiot,' she muttered under her breath. 'What did you go and say that for? Why couldn't you just say thank you very much, Daniel, what a lovely idea, when you know it's what you really want to do?'

Because she'd spent too many years sidestepping such invitations from doctors who seemed to think that a very ordinary nurse like her ought to be so grateful to have caught his notice that, after the meal, she'd automatically invite him to stay the night.

She had no illusions about her own lack of attractions—she'd had that brought home to her in no uncertain way over ten years ago.

But she knew that Daniel was different. She'd had evidence of the fact right from the first time that they'd worked together, and her respect for him was growing daily.

She'd overheard him telling Maddie that he wanted to be her friend, but instead of responding to his invitation as a friend she'd treated him like an unwanted suitor.

That was the problem.

Not that he was a suitor, because she realised he would never be that. No, the problem was that he wasn't unwanted.

In fact, the more she saw of him, the more she realised she *did* want him, in spite of her resolve and in spite of the fact that there could never be a permanent commitment between them.

Sarian was grabbing a chance at a cup of coffee during a brief lull when the phone rang almost beside her.

'Hello? Lizzie's...I mean, St Elizabeth's Hospital. Can I help you?' She had no idea how to answer, as this wasn't the internal line she was accustomed to.

'I hope so. Is that the accident and emergency department?' asked a deep voice.

'That's right, but this isn't the number you have to ring for appointments, or anything.'

'Actually, I'm trying to contact a friend of mine. Easy Burr? He's a registrar on A and E.'

Easy...?

'Oh, you mean Daniel. If you can hang on a minute…'

She turned to ask if anyone knew where Daniel was, and almost came face to face with him.

'For me?' he asked, holding his hand out.

'If your name's Easy Burr, yes,' she said, making sure she handed the phone over without touching him.

For a moment she thought of abandoning her peaceful cup of coffee—it wouldn't be nearly as peaceful with the object of her turmoil just feet away from her.

Common sense and good Welsh grit made her determined to stick it out and she sat herself back in a slightly tatty but surprisingly comfortable chair.

Of course, the fact that she could overhear at least one half of Daniel's conversation had absolutely nothing to do with her decision to stay put. Finding out that his nickname was Easy had given her enough to think about.

Or, was it a nickname of a nickname? Had it started off as easygoing, for example? It would certainly be appropriate. He'd hardly batted an eye when she'd refused his invitation, as if her reply hadn't really mattered.

'Hey, Rob! That's great! Congratulations!' Daniel said exuberantly, shattering Sarian's transparent attempt at ignoring him. 'So when will you be arriving?'

As she watched his smile dimmed and his expression grew more serious.

'Is this the last operation or will there be more?' he said, tantalising Sarian with yet more half-revealed mysteries. 'Give her my love and tell her I'll be in to visit her as soon as she arrives. Have you sorted out somewhere to live yet?'

There was another break while he listened to his

friend, but Sarian was too interested in watching the changing parade of expressions across Daniel's face. She didn't think she'd ever seen him so unguarded, except when he was dealing with their little patients.

'You could stay with me until you get yourself organised,' he was offering as she tuned back into the conversation. 'It'll give you and Angel some time to find what you want.'

The discussion ended with a repeat of his congratulations before he turned to face the rest of the room.

'Hey, you lot. The new specialist registrar for A and E has been appointed,' he announced to a suddenly riveted audience. 'His name is Robert Oliver.'

'Is he the candidate you already know?' someone asked. Sarian thought from the accented voice that it was probably Spiro Kristakis, their anaesthetist.

'That's the one,' Daniel confirmed with a beaming smile. 'We did our training together.'

'Well, surely, as you were on the interviewing panel, you should already have known he was getting the job?'

'Because we've been friends for so long, I notified them of the friendship and excused myself from interviewing him,' Daniel explained. 'Until just now, I didn't know the offer had gone out, or that Rob had accepted.'

The room dissolved into chaos as one half peppered him with more questions while the rest tried to return to their own conversations.

Sarian stayed silent. If she'd understood what she'd overheard correctly, she'd be meeting Robert Oliver sooner than most when he moved in with Daniel. The same Daniel who apparently answered to the name 'Easy'…

*　　*　　*

'Maddie!' Sarian called as she let herself into the flat. 'What have you been cooking? The whole house smells gorgeous as soon as you come in the door.'

Silence. Not a sign of movement anywhere.

'Maddie?'

Sarian frowned as she stood in the middle of the sitting room and absent-mindedly began to undo her long jacket ready to pile her belongings on the end of the settee-cum-bed.

Where could she be? She'd said she was going to do the cooking tonight as she was on day off, and Sarian was going to return the favour tomorrow.

Perhaps she'd taken a load of washing downstairs?

Sarian wandered into the compact kitchen in search of simmering pots and pans but there was nothing cooking. The room smelled wonderful but the cooker wasn't even switched on.

But there *was* a piece of paper with her name written on the outside in large letters, and it was attached to the door of the fridge by a smiley frog magnet.

Sarian couldn't help smiling back at it. The first time she'd seen it Maddie had told her that one day, her frog was going to turn into the perfect handsome prince, or perhaps find one for her.

. She started to slide the paper out from under it, then changed her mind and lifted it up to press a kiss to his wide-mouthed grin.

'Not turned into a prince yet, I see,' she commented as she unfolded the paper and read the message.

Sarian groaned.

What was Maddie up to?

'Dinner's upstairs. Come and get it,' it said succinctly.

After the embarrassment of turning down his invitation, she'd been dreading seeing him. Now, she was going to end up eating with him anyway. At least, with Maddie there, she wasn't going to have to face Daniel alone.

This was getting to be a habit. First, the kiss last night followed by the ordeal of facing him this morning; now she was going through the same thing all over again after turning down his invitation for a meal.

She wondered if he would appreciate the irony of the fact that Maddie's generosity meant she would be dining with him after all?

For just a moment she contemplated changing again out of her simple navy jeans and burgundy sweatshirt outfit into something that would give her a little more of a boost to her confidence, then dismissed the idea.

'You'll never make a silk purse out of a sow's ear,' her grandmother used to say. And, 'To thine own self be true.' Well, she'd long ago accepted that she would never bowl anybody over with her beauty, so she might as well admit that she was just a jeans-and-sweatshirt sort of person.

'I'll brush my hair and wash my hands, but that's it,' she muttered. It was only a meal with friends, after all...

'About time!' Maddie exclaimed, a steaming plate full of food balanced between both hands, when Sarian finally knocked on Daniel's door. 'Come on in. Everything's ready.'

It was the first time that Sarian had ventured up to Daniel's domain and she stood just inside the door and gazed around.

From the size of it, it looked as if his flat must be the only one on this floor.

The room she was standing in was a strange shape,

with the pale walls sloping in a series of angles to meet the vaulted timber-clad ceiling.

The floor, too, was honey-coloured timber, the expanse only broken by a vaguely Persian-looking carpet square of rich burgundy and navy set against a cream background. The furniture was cream, too—what there was of it—and the whole feeling of the room was clean and spare but strangely inviting.

Sarian was so busy looking around that she didn't realise that Maddie was disappearing out of the door until she heard it shut behind her.

'Maddie?' she called after her, but all she heard was the sound of swiftly retreating feet.

'She's taken her share with her,' Daniel said quietly. 'The option's open if you want to do the same.'

At the sound of his voice Sarian's pulse went wild and she had to pause a second to gather her composure around her before she slowly turned round.

He was standing in the doorway at the opposite end of the room leaning one shoulder against the frame. The way his arms were folded across the expanse of cream knitted jumper made him look very relaxed, but that wasn't true of the wary expression he couldn't hide in his eyes.

Sarian wondered fleetingly when she'd learned to read him so well, but that wasn't as important as dealing with the emotions he was revealing.

Her own trepidation seemed to have disappeared as soon as she'd realised he was feeling the same way.

'Is mine served out too?' she asked softly, beginning to walk the length of the room towards him and hoping he couldn't tell that she was shaking all over.

She had a strange feeling that what happened in this room over the next few moments could decide the whole course of her life…or at least her happiness for the foreseeable future.

'It wouldn't take long,' he replied, his face growing suddenly blank as he straightened away from the door frame and began to turn away from her.

'Good. I've been smelling whatever it is since I stood on the front doorstep trying to find my key, and I'm starving,' she said. 'Where are we going to eat it?'

He turned his head almost in slow motion to look back at her, as if he couldn't really believe what he'd just heard. Suddenly her words seemed to register properly and she was treated to one of those rare heartfelt smiles that could easily send her into orbit.

'How about there?' He pointed to a small table set in front of a window whose window sill doubled as a seat on one side of the table.

'Perfect,' she declared. 'Where do you keep the cutlery?'

The next few minutes of bustle demolished the last of the awkwardness between them as Daniel handed her handfuls of cutlery or directed her to the right cupboard to find the glasses.

'This is gorgeous,' Sarian declared with her first mouthful. 'It's very much like that spicy curry Maddie likes making, but there's definitely something different about it.'

'She said you didn't like it very hot.'

'Quite right. I've far too much respect for my taste-buds to singe them unnecessarily,' she agreed. 'But I love the mixture of spices in here. It's a lovely balance so none of them is overpowering. You can taste them all.'

'I thank you, with all due humility,' he said with a

return of his wicked grin. 'I've always loved experimenting with herbs and so on.'

'Why?'

'Because even a slight change in the balance of flavours can make such a difference to the finished—'

'No, Daniel. I mean why did you arrange this?' She gestured first between the two of them, sitting side by side as they were, looking out over the table at the strings of lights that marked the surrounding streets, then widened the gesture to include the meal and their immediate surroundings.

'Because you wouldn't go out with me,' he said simply, dropping his eyes to watch his hand as he traced the rim of his glass with the tip of one lean finger.

'So you and Maddie cooked all this up between you—excuse the pun—to force me to go out with you?'

'Ah, but you haven't "gone out with me",' he pointed out virtuously, obviously trying to fight a wicked grin. 'Technically, we're still at home.'

'Pedant,' she scorned, but inside she was very touched that he would have wanted to make her change her mind. Wanted it enough to find a way around her objections.

But why?

For the rest of their very pleasant evening, one small corner of her brain was carefully sifting everything he said, looking for clues.

She found none while they finished their leisurely meal, talking continuously about everything under the sun. She found none when she insisted on helping with the washing-up, either, too busy laughing and retaliating when he flicked froth at her.

By the time she finally admitted it was time to go

back to her own flat so she wouldn't disturb Maggie by coming in late, she'd given up looking for clues to his unexpected desire for her company. She'd finally been able to relax as if there were no difference between spending time with him and spending time with Maddie...well, almost no difference...

True to his usual gentlemanly instincts, Daniel insisted that he was going to escort her home. Sarian thought nothing of it until he paused just inside his own front door to look down into her uplifted face.

It was getting late and the house was silent apart from the sounds of passing traffic.

Sarian could almost wish that there was a brass band going past to hide the sudden sound of her heart trying to beat its way out of her chest.

As it was, it was quiet enough that she could hear the slightly unsteady rhythm of Daniel's breathing and she realised that it almost matched hers.

'Sarian,' he whispered, seeming to savour the sound of her name. He lifted one hand to smooth a stray spiral of hair away from her forehead and lingered to trace the outline of her jaw.

With the soft lighting concentrated on the other side of the room there were shadows at this end, but she could still see the sharp gleam of those impossibly green eyes as he scanned her face.

'Oh, hell,' he breathed as he reached for her and wrapped both arms around her.

It was several aeons before he lifted his head and broke the searing contact between their lips, but it was still too soon for Sarian.

She was leaning bonelessly against him as he in turn leant against his front door, and she couldn't have moved away if her life depended on it.

He seemed to feel the same way because as she forced her eyes open she was just in time to see his head angling towards hers again.

'I really have to stop doing this,' he murmured against her lips, his voice hoarse and almost disjointed as he changed the angle for a deeper contact.

'Yes, you really do,' she murmured and tried reluctantly to force herself to draw away. 'In a minute…'

Sarian adjusted the speed of the drip and turned towards the translator.

'Could you make sure that Mr and Mrs Patel understand that their baby was just very badly dehydrated?' she asked with another glance at the young couple.

Mrs Patel had hardly said a thing since she'd accompanied her husband and tiny child into the A and E department. She'd just been sitting silently beside her eight-week-old son crying a steady stream of tears.

'Tell her it was only because of the sickness and diarrhoea,' she continued when the first flurry of conversation halted. 'The liquid going down the tube into his arm is mostly water to put back what he's lost.'

She heard footsteps behind her and half turned to glance over her shoulder just as Daniel arrived.

'Have the results come back about his electrolyte levels?' he asked, picking up Ravi's free hand and pinching the skin gently to see how quickly and easily it returned to normal. Sarian noted that it was still tending to stay 'tented' for a moment, indicating that his fluid levels were still too low.

'The results are due back any minute, but I can already see an improvement in him,' she said.

'Have you come up with any possible causes for the vomiting and diarrhoea?' he asked, his voice slightly preoccupied as he listened to little Ravi's heartbeat and compared his findings with the previous figures on his case notes. He'd had to leave Sarian to deal with the non-English-speaking Patel family until the translator could arrive to ask for the answers to their essential questions.

'One possibility seems to be a wheat allergy,' she said. 'Apparently, Mrs Patel recently started giving Ravi a little cereal in his midday bottle. The problem started at about the same time.'

'Good detective work. I hope you're right because that's a lot simpler for us to deal with than an infection, especially when they're this small.'

'Not quite so easy for his mother to deal with once he gets big enough to demand cakes, biscuits and pastries,' she pointed out. 'If we *have* got the right diagnosis I'll have to get the interpreter to find out about the translations of the coeliac disease dietary advice leaflets.'

'In the meantime, it would be an idea if you could organise some tea or coffee for Mr and Mrs Patel,' Daniel suggested with a compassionate glance in their direction. 'It's bad enough having a sick child, but to be unable to ask his doctor any questions except through a third person must be a nightmare.'

The young couple seemed quite surprised when the offer of cups of tea was translated, and it was amazing how much less stressed they seemed to be once they'd had a drink. Whether it was the sheer ordinariness of the activity that broke the tension, Sarian didn't know, but she'd seen it happen so often that it didn't do to discount its effectiveness. At least Mrs Patel had stopped crying.

Within an hour it looked as if Ravi was well on his

way to recovery and Sarian had even surprised a smile out of his mother when she'd tickled his little chin and made him smile.

'It's amazing how quickly they can pick up when it's just dehydration,' she said, gratefully accepting a large mug of coffee of her own in the relative peace of the staff room.

'Just like the rest of us,' Daniel said wryly as he toasted her with his own mug. 'I was reading something the other day that maintained that most of us are sub-clinically dehydrated most of the time. It said that every adult should drink at least two litres a day, but that didn't include any tea, coffee, fizzy drinks or alcoholic drinks which all have diuretic actions.'

Sarian tried to work out exactly how much water and fruit juice she would have to drink if she were to achieve the recommended level.

'Who's cooking tonight?' Daniel asked suddenly and her calculations disintegrated.

'We're fending for ourselves tonight,' she explained. 'Maddie's going out to the multiplex cinema to see that Mel Gibson film they've all been talking about.'

'Didn't you want to go too? He's one of the big cinema heartthrobs, isn't he?' he teased.

'I've never really followed that very much,' she said quietly, thinking back briefly over the many evenings when she'd opted to stay in rather than risk being the odd one out in an off-duty group of fun-loving colleagues.

'Not even as a teenager? I bet you and Maddie were proper little hellions when you were at boarding-school together.'

Sarian remembered how much she'd hated being at

boarding-school and the thought must have shown itself on her face.

'What did I say?' he prompted quietly, leaning forward to give their conversation a little more privacy. 'I thought you and Maddie were good friends from those days but, just then, it looked as if I'd brought up an unhappy time.'

Sarian smiled wryly.

'My friendship with Maddie was the only good part about those years,' she said in a low voice. 'If it hadn't been for her, I don't know what would have happened. And as for her support after I left school...'

She broke off, unwilling to get into such personal things in such a public place.

'Suffice it to say that if it weren't for Maddie, it wouldn't be Junior Sister Sarian Williams sitting here now.'

'She persuaded you to go in for nursing?'

'She persuaded me that anything was better than life on the dole and then badgered me until I got the qualifications I needed to apply for a place to do my nursing training.'

He was listening with a slight frown pleating his forehead. 'But, if you went to the same school, how come you didn't come out with good enough results to get there first time?'

'A combination of reasons,' she admitted in a low voice full of tired old regrets. 'Mostly to do with my own short-sighted stupidity and *naïveté*. In other words, I deliberately set out to fail my exams so my parents couldn't force me into their idea of a suitable profession. I wanted them to accept me for the person I was, not for the person they wanted me to be or the reflected glory they could bask in. Needless to say, I ended up cutting off my nose to spite my face, because they washed their hands of me.'

He shook his head, apparently unable to fathom the reasoning behind her actions.

'I went about things in exactly the opposite way,' he said quietly, and the way he was concentrating on tracing the pattern on the outside of his mug told Sarian that he was avoiding meeting her gaze. 'Once I realised that I'd got a good brain, I worked out what I really wanted to do. I knew I'd never get a second shot at it so I slogged myself to a standstill to get there.'

He paused for a moment and she could almost hear the silent debate going on inside his head as he decided whether to say any more.

She concentrated on staying very still, not saying a word in case he stopped speaking.

'Mostly,' he continued, his voice taking on a scratchy quality as though the words were being dredged up from painful places, 'mostly, it was because I was utterly determined to get away from my parents.'

Sarian didn't quite know what to say.

Anyway, the staff room was hardly the right place for anyone to bare their soul. Too many people were willing to spread gossip, and the last thing either of them needed was to have their secrets made the stuff of common knowledge.

It was just a shame that the first time Daniel had ever given her a glimpse into his private side, it should be somewhere where it was impossible to ask questions.

It would have been different if they'd been alone together…sharing a meal, perhaps…

She drew in a steadying breath and mentally crossed her fingers before she made her suggestion, fully aware that it was the first time she'd ever dared to issue such an invitation...or ever wanted to.

'Do you feel brave enough to chance my cooking?'

CHAPTER EIGHT

DANIEL leant back in the middle of his oversized settee and watched Sarian bustling around.

In spite of the reservations of a lifetime, there was something very *right* about the feelings it gave him, having her up here in his flat again.

A strange longing curled through him like smoke from a chimney spiralling up into frosty winter air. It wasn't something he'd felt before so he dismissed it firmly, concentrating on the unexpected situation developing right in front of him.

After her wariness around him he'd been surprised and delighted that she'd offered to cook him a meal and he'd jumped at the chance. It had taken some very quick creative thinking on his part to find some excuse for her to prepare it in his kitchen.

He'd offered to help—what single man could afford not to learn to fend for himself, especially one like him who had no intention of marrying?—but she'd delighted him by bossily delegating him to setting the table and keeping her supplied with conversation.

It was strange when he thought about how many changes he'd seen in her since they'd met.

He'd only known her since the end of October... He couldn't help smiling when he remembered her costumed double-act with Maddie a couple of days later, and the fun they'd had with their make-up. He'd been amazed when he'd realised that she genuinely didn't seem to know that her beauty shone through even her crone's guise.

And she *was* beautiful, he thought, his eyes never leaving her as she stirred something vigorously, every inch of her slender body shown off to perfection in the softly draped dress she'd donned for the occasion. It was high-necked and covered her all the way to her wrists and halfway down her calves but the supple fabric seemed to enhance rather than hide her figure.

She was slim and elegant, her legs looking impossibly long in the heeled shoes she'd worn when she'd arrived. They'd been discarded now, and she was padding around in her stockings with an easy familiarity that surprised him.

It shouldn't have. She seemed to have the amazing ability, once she got past that strange reticence, of being able to fit in almost anywhere.

In A and E, for example, she had made friends with almost everyone on the staff. At first that could have been put down to their appreciation of her excellent professional standards and her willingness to work hard, but he'd soon realised that it was because people were responding to the fact that she was just genuinely nice, right through.

It was probably because he had secrets, too, that he'd recognised the shadows in her eyes for what they were. Because of this, he had known that it would take time and quiet persistence before she would let those last barriers down, and at last it seemed as if it was working.

He remembered the apprehensive woman who had tried to wriggle out of going to something as unthreatening as the Halloween disco, and had grown tense every time he'd come within yards of her or even thrown a teasing remark. Who would have thought that, just weeks later, she would be in his flat humming happily as she peered at something under the grill?

He couldn't stop looking at her and the way the dark sapphire of her dress set off her pale hair to perfection, making it look almost ethereal as the curls tumbled freely over her shoulders.

He'd known from the first moment she'd looked up at him that her eyes were grey, but he hadn't realised exactly how many shades of grey they could be until he'd begun watching them. This evening, as she'd carried an armful of ingredients into his flat, they'd been almost silvery with animation and anticipation and he knew that when he teased her about her loyalty to her Welsh heritage they almost shot sparks at him.

But he couldn't help thinking about the soft grey of a dove's breast he'd seen when she'd gazed up at him in the aftermath of that kiss.

He shook his head in self-disgust.

Get a grip, man. It was only a kiss…just a simple goodnight kiss…nothing special…

Except it *had* been special in a way that he still hadn't been able to fathom… And if he kept thinking about it while he was sitting here watching her bustling about in his flat, he wasn't going to be able to get up and walk to the table without embarrassing them both.

'What did I do wrong?' Sarian whispered miserably as she pulled the covers up over her head.

The meal had been beautiful, even though she said so herself. The salmon steaks had been cooked to perfection, the Hollandaise sauce had been made from scratch and had been as smooth as silk, and there hadn't been a single limp, overcooked vegetable in sight.

The conversation had flowed as easily as the bottle of white wine Daniel had produced and his praise of the lemon, cream and sherry concoction she'd whisked up for dessert had made her blush.

Their kisses had made her blush, too, especially when he'd lain down beside her on the settee and she'd realised that he'd become aroused.

Surprise had frozen her for a moment when she'd realised the effect she'd had on him. For just that moment she'd been afraid that old fears and insecurities would take over once more, but it hadn't happened.

This was Daniel, her friend, she'd realised with a flood of relief as she'd tightened her arms around him and offered her mouth. Daniel was the man who was so patient and gentle that, in a matter of weeks, he had overcome years of fear and distrust and changed them to…love…?

As if his inbuilt radar had detected the word even in her thoughts, suddenly it had been Daniel's turn to freeze. In the blink of an eye he'd been halfway across the room, his broad back turned to her as he'd apologised.

She'd stared at him in dismay for several stunned seconds, but he'd remained silent, apparently riveted by the view out of the window with his hands fisted in his trouser pockets and his cream shirt looking decidedly crumpled.

In minutes he'd gathered himself together and she'd been handed her discarded shoes and ushered to the door. This time there'd been no pause for a blood-stirring kiss, nor the offer of an escort to her door.

She hadn't even been able to ask him what had gone wrong.

She'd been achingly aware that he'd stood silently watching from the top of the stairs until she'd been safely home, but from the moment he'd leapt off the settee his face had been completely closed to her.

'Hello, Justin, what have you been up to?' Sarian asked as she followed the wheelchair through to one of the larger cubicles.

'Fighting with my brother,' he announced with a grimace, cradling one arm against his body, and squeaked as his father carefully lifted him up onto the bed.

His distinctive diminutive shape told her that he was suffering from brittle bones disease, and he would be well used to the pain of yet another broken bone.

'So, what were you fighting about?' Between them, she and Justin's mother were carefully removing the youngster's clothes. Sarian noticed that, in spite of the fact that they were obviously in the colours of the local football team, they had been carefully chosen for ease of removal. She knew that sometimes even a moment's inattention when putting a fragile arm into a sleeve could result in a fracture.

'I wanted to watch the football and he kept changing the channel on the TV, so I hit him.'

'Not a very clever thing to do,' Sarian pointed out, stifling her own wince when she saw him grimace at an incautious movement.

'He's got his own TV, anyway, so I don't see why he should come in and interfere with mine,' he said with a spirited lift of his chin. 'And now I don't know whether it's going to stop me having my operation next week.'

'You were going to be coming into St Elizabeth's? What were you having done?' She made a note to look up the details on the computer.

'They were going to be putting a thing up the centre of the bones in my arm to make it straighter and so it wouldn't keep getting broken,' he explained. 'It was supposed to be done so I could have the cast off before Christmas.'

While he'd been speaking, Daniel had arrived to have a look, but in spite of the fact he spent some time talking to Justin and his parents he didn't once glance in Sarian's direction.

It had been the same way ever since she'd arrived for work, and she was getting fed up with it.

In a minute her Welsh blood was going to overcome her common sense and she was going to tell him what she thought of his manners.

In the meantime, she had a little boy to take care of, and Daniel wanted him taken for an X-ray.

'Shall I see who's free to come down from Orthopaedics?' she asked Daniel quietly.

'Yes, please. And see if you can find out the details about his admission at the same time.'

His tone was perfectly polite—probably because there were people in the cubicle with them—but he hadn't so much as glanced at her and his voice had all the warmth of yesterday's rice pudding.

Sarian pushed the wheelchair through the department to the small waiting area outside the X-ray room and left Justin and his family waiting while she returned to the nurses' station to access his file on the computer.

By the time the orthopaedic consultant arrived, Justin had returned to the cubicle with yet another set of X-rays to add to his bulging file.

'Hey, you, what did I tell you about hitting your brother?' Peter Harding, who had replaced Lucas Morrison, said with a shake of his head, then held one of the X-ray plates up.

'What's he done this time? Is it going to stop him having the operation?' Justin's mother's voice was full of the sort of weary anxiety that spoke of many such visits since her little son had been born.

'Actually, looking at the break, I think the best thing will be if I take him up to theatre as soon as I can get it arranged,' the orthopaedic consultant said with a wry smile. 'It looks as if Justin's actually done himself a favour this time, and made it worthwhile bringing his operation forward. What the hospital beds manager is going to say, I don't know—probably tell me she's going to have to put your bed in the broom cupboard.'

Justin giggled and his parents looked immeasurably brighter that he hadn't ruined the planned operation.

While Daniel and Peter headed out of the cubicle Sarian stayed with the family and was soon in the middle of a family row.

'I've told you before not to torment Justin,' his father said to Charlie, waving a finger under his other son's nose. 'And as for you...'

Justin's pixie face screwed up into a put-upon expression. 'Well, it was my TV. He only does it because he knows I can't fight him for the channel changer.'

'Yeah, but you only wanted to watch the football...' his brother chimed in.

'But, Justin, you know you shouldn't hit your brother,' his mother began.

Sarian could see that, in a minute, she might end up with more than one bone broken, and the noise level was rising by the second.

'Excuse me,' she began in ringing tones. 'Do any of you read Chinese?'

There was a startled silence as they all turned and stared at her.

'Chinese?' they said, almost in unison.

'Yes. The Chinese have a saying that the person who strikes the first blow has just lost the argument.'

She paused for a moment, watching their puzzled expressions before she spoke directly to Justin.

'What I think it means is this. The next time Charlie comes in and changes the channel on your TV when you don't want him to, don't hit him. All you have to do is start talking.'

'Talking about what?' Justin demanded.

'Anything.' Sarian waved her arms. 'Everything. Just keep talking and talking until he gets so cross that he can't hear his programme that he'll go and watch his own TV.'

'Hey! Neat!' Justin crowed.

'Oh, no!' his father groaned theatrically. 'Do you know what you've just done, Sister? This lad could win an Olympic medal for talking non-stop.'

'At least, if he drives you all mad, he won't break any bones doing it,' Sarian pointed out with a grin.

There were several other broken bones to deal with during that shift, but none as complicated as Justin's.

Two were broken arms with almost identical Colles' fractures, both needing lots of sympathy and a trip to the plaster room.

One was a broken finger that had been trapped in a car door and the sling protecting the injured digit was far more impressive than the strapping holding it to its neighbour for support.

Within half an hour, the four-year-old was on her

way out of A and E carrying a certificate proclaiming her bravery, and had promised to colour the pictures on it as soon as she got home.

'Another satisfied customer?' asked Jenny Barber when Sarian returned to the nurses' station for her next patient. 'Bet it doesn't stop her playing with car doors any more than it did with *my* daughter. Luckily she only bruised hers and lost the nail'

'How old is she?' Sarian asked suddenly. She knew from things that Maddie had told her about their colleagues that Jenny had married part-way through her training. Once her children had been beyond the baby stage, she'd returned to complete her training, but Sarian was ashamed to realise that she'd hardly bothered to find out any more. It had become a habit to skate over other people's lives, probably so that they wouldn't take it as an invitation to ask about her own.

'She's just over five and full of herself because she started ''real'' school in September.' Jenny pulled a face. 'Sometimes I wonder if I've done the right thing by coming back to finish my training while she's so little. I'm missing so much of her growing up.'

'Could you face staying home twenty-four hours a day just for an after-school conversation with a five-year-old who'd rather be watching TV?' Sarian asked. 'And what about the financial aspects?'

'You're right,' Jenny conceded. 'I really enjoy nursing most of the time, and I don't know how we'd cope without the money.'

'If you're really concerned that your shifts are too disruptive for your daughter, perhaps you could swap to nights full-time, or do a job share with another mum, so you can get the best of both worlds.'

'Full-time nights would certainly help to stop me

getting pregnant again,' Jenny joked. 'I'd probably never see my husband.'

There were more patients waiting for both of them and as they set off in opposite directions Sarian had a better appreciation of the problems married nurses faced once they had children. Because she'd never intended marrying she'd just never thought about it before.

For just a split second she found herself wondering what it would be like to finish her shift knowing she was going to go home and find Daniel waiting for her.

It was harder than she would have liked to banish the image and it left her with a strange hollow feeling inside when she reminded herself that it was something that could never happen.

Still, the fact that neither of them had any intention of having a serious relationship was no excuse for his behaviour last night.

When she'd first met him, she'd been very wary of his open charm. As she'd got to know him better, she'd gradually realised that, while the charm was genuine, it was also a camouflage for hidden scars.

For him to have treated her so abruptly last night meant that she must have done or said something to upset him. Perhaps it was something that trespassed too close to those hidden scars.

Or was she completely off course?

Unless she could pin the wretched man down, she was never going to be able to find out and, if necessary, apologise.

Her frustration grew by the hour as Daniel successfully avoided any but the most superficial contact with her.

After the recent weeks, when he'd thoroughly lived

up to his name and stuck to her like a burr, it felt almost like an amputation not to have him nearby.

By the time she was ready to go home and found out that he'd left not five minutes earlier, she started to steam.

All the way home she rehearsed what she was going to say when she confronted him…and confront him she would.

The journey seemed to be over in a flash with no time to notice whether it was wet or dry. She made just a brief detour to her own front door, barely opening it wide enough to dump her belongings before she started to pull it shut again.

At the last moment, she caught sight of Daniel's key hung up on the corner of the frame of the mirror by the phone and with an unholy grin she snatched it up.

Her memories of the last time she'd climbed these stairs, just last night with her arms full of ingredients for the meal she'd been going to cook for him, couldn't be more different from her feelings now.

She paused briefly outside his door and, for the space of a single second, contemplated the wisdom of knocking first, then dismissed it in a blaze of Welsh ire and determination.

Inserting the key in the lock, she gave it a firm twist and thrust the door open, striding into the room without giving herself a chance to chicken out.

A sharply drawn breath drew her eyes across to the other side of the room where Daniel was just emerging from the bathroom with nothing more than a towel in his hand.

Sarian was shocked into silence by her first view of all his naked glory but when he whirled away from her she couldn't help the cry of compassion when she saw the myriad welts of scars criss-crossing his back.

'Oh, Daniel, what happened?' she demanded softly, hardly aware she'd moved across the room until she reached her hand out towards him.

'Don't.'

The single word froze her hand in mid-reach.

'Daniel...' She ached for him, suddenly wondering if this was the reason he'd pulled away from her yesterday. They looked like old scars, but he was obviously painfully aware of them.

'You shouldn't be here,' he said gruffly as he strode back into the bathroom.

When he swung the door closed, Sarian wondered if he was going to lock the door until she left, but he emerged moments later tightening the belt of a burgundy towelling dressing gown around his waist.

'What do you want?' he demanded, the wash of colour across his cheek-bones and the way he looked anywhere but at her telling her of his mortification.

For a moment she almost turned in ignominious retreat but something—some half-seen flicker in his expression—told her that it was exactly what he was expecting her to do.

'We need to talk,' she declared, taking the offensive.

'There's nothing to talk about,' he countered instantly, folding his arms across his chest in a blatantly defensive gesture before he realised what he'd done and dropped them by his sides.

'Fine. You don't want to say anything so that leaves the floor clear for me to get some things off my chest.'

She was shaking with nerves but, thank goodness, there didn't seem to be any sign of it in her voice. Her legs were a different matter and, because she needed to sit down before she fell down, she turned and marched the few steps required to take her to the settee.

For one horrible moment she wondered if the memories of what they'd done here just a few hours ago were going to rob her of her determination, but they actually stiffened her backbone.

'If we're going to be able to work together properly we need to clear the air,' she began firmly, sitting herself on one end of the settee.

She looked across at him and waited for him to speak but he remained stubbornly silent.

'For heaven's sake, Daniel, we're both adults,' she exclaimed, frustrated by his obstinacy. 'We had an enjoyable meal last night with plenty of conversation and lots of laughter, and then we kissed each other and that was very...very nice, too.'

She had to pause to catch her breath. She'd nearly lost her nerve then, when she'd had to find a word to describe what his kisses had meant to her. Only the memory of his less than enthralled reaction had made her use caution.

'Nice?' The strange tone in his voice snapped her eyes up to him in a hurry. 'Nice?' he repeated, clearly incensed as he strode towards her, coming to a halt right in front of her with his fists planted on his hips. 'We share kisses that damn near cause spontaneous combustion and you say they were *nice*?'

He reached down to grasp her firmly by her elbows and lifted her out of the seat in one powerful movement.

Her feet hardly touched the floor when he wrapped his arms around her and his head swooped down.

'I'll show you *nice*,' he muttered against her lips just before his kiss whirled her into oblivion.

It was a long time before he allowed her to surface for air and by that time they were both entwined on the settee again.

'I see what you mean about the spontaneous combustion,' she whispered weakly, her brain slowly beginning to unscramble itself. 'But, if you enjoyed it too, why did you stop last night? Why were you so *angry* with me?'

'I wasn't angry with you. I was angry with myself,' he said heavily as he began to disentangle himself.

'Why?' Stubbornly, she refused to release him, certain that he was trying to put emotional as well as physical distance between them at the same time.

'Sarian, it's no good,' he said, giving up the fight and letting his head drop back so that he was staring up into the timber-clad cathedral ceiling. 'I'll never be what you need. I don't know all the things I need to know to make you happy.'

'Well, you were certainly making a good start just now,' she began in a shaky attempt at humour. She rolled towards him and propped her head on one hand so that she could look down at his face, hoping to catch a glimpse of that wicked grin of his.

All she saw in his beautiful green eyes were shadows and misery, so she abandoned levity and stuck to the unadorned truth. 'Oh, Daniel, don't you know that you're *exactly* what I need?'

Nervously taking the initiative for the first time in her life, she framed his face with her hands and lowered her lips to his.

For endless moments he lay still and unresponsive, even when she tilted her head to deepen the contact. She was just about to retreat in utter humiliation when he moved, his fingers suddenly spearing through her hair as he took control.

'Oh, Sarian, I hope you mean that,' he muttered between frantic kisses. 'I think I'd die if you changed your mind now.'

Change her mind? What mind? His kisses had turned it to mush then vaporised it, leaving only a body controlled by love and desire.

Time ceased to have any meaning as their kisses grew deeper, their hands impatient with the confines of clothing as they began to explore.

Old insecurities rose up and Sarian was almost paralysed by shyness when Daniel peeled her uniform off her, leaving her wearing only her plain white underwear.

'Beautiful,' he murmured fervently, the stroke of his eyes over her slender curves and hollows almost as potent as his hands. 'Oh, Sarian, you're so beautiful.'

His hand was trembling as he tried to release the catch on her bra and the momentary pause and the novelty of the situation reminded her that there was something important that she needed to tell him.

'Daniel,' she whispered, closing her eyes so that she could pretend she was having this conversation in the dark. 'I need to…there's something I should… You should…'

Her halting progress obviously caught his attention because, in the space of a second, he completely stopped what he was doing.

Sarian forced her eyes open and caught a glimpse of the desolation he swiftly hid.

'You want me to stop,' he said in a resigned voice and rolled away from her, almost falling onto the floor as he came perilously close to the edge of the settee.

'No!' Sarian grabbed for him, both to stop him leaving her and to prevent his undignified descent. 'No, I don't want you to stop, it's just… Could we…could we take this a bit…slowly?'

'Oh, Sarian.' Daniel gave a breathless chuckle as he returned her hug. 'If you're sure you want to continue, let's go somewhere just a bit more comfortable and you can take this as slowly as you like. In fact, I'm putting you in charge of everything.'

'Oh, but…' Sarian paused. How was she going to tell him that if she was in charge they might never achieve anything?

She squeaked when he swung her up into his arms and carried her through into his softly lit bedroom, the only room she hadn't seen before.

The plain, no-nonsense décor steadied her nerves again. The soft patina of the wooden floor was broken by a creamy rug either side of the king-size divan bed and the bed itself boasted an ordinary duvet. It was all so typical of the Daniel she had come to know and love that all embarrassment disappeared.

'Actually, Daniel, that might not be a very good idea because I've no idea how to…please you. It's the first time that—'

'Shh!' He touched gentle fingertips to her lips. 'This is a first time for both of us, so you'll have to tell me what you like, and I'll tell you. Nice and easy,' he promised, obviously forgetting his recent objection to the word. 'Nice and easy.'

In spite of his bracing words she noticed that he hesitated just for a moment before he reached for the belt barely holding his robe together and shrugged out of it, letting it fall in a heap at his bare feet.

'First, I'd like to see you without this,' he whispered,

reaching for her bra again and lightly tracing the curve as fabric met flesh.

This time the catch released first time and when she saw the way his pupils dilated at the sight of her naked breasts she knew that he truly found her beautiful.

'Touch me,' he pleaded softly, and when she hesitated, uncertain what he wanted, he took both her hands in his and placed them flat on his chest.

He felt so warm, she thought as she absorbed the new sensations. So warm and so solid, with silky tawny hairs marching in a swathe between dark coppery nipples…nipples that responded to her tentative exploration by tightening into little knots. Little knots that…that made him groan and trap her hands under his.

'Fair's fair,' he muttered hoarsely as he placed her hands by her sides. 'You torment me and I'll torment you.'

He lifted cupped hands to cradle her and tease her but when he lowered his mouth to suckle her she cried out.

'Too much?' he asked, pausing immediately.

'Only…' She gasped for air. 'Only if you expect me to go on standing. My knees…'

With a wicked smile he scooped her up in his arms again and tumbled her onto the bed, quickly following her down.

'Ready?' he whispered, and began all over again.

'You should have told me,' Daniel said fiercely, his body still trembling with the after-effects of passion as he glared down at her. 'By the time I realised you were a virgin…'

'It was too late,' Sarian finished for him, feeling a

Cheshire-cat grin creeping over her face. 'Anyway, what difference would it have made? You wanted to make love to me and I wanted to make love to you...'

A sudden thought stopped her in her tracks.

'Unless...unless you didn't enjoy it?' she finished hesitantly.

'Not enjoy it?' He gave a short exasperated laugh and pressed a stormy kiss to her lips. 'How could I *not* enjoy it? It was so much more than my wildest imaginings. All these years I've wondered...'

He stopped suddenly and shook his head, his mouth pressed tightly shut as though to prevent any more words escaping.

Sarian felt the sudden tension fill his body and rapidly replayed his words.

'All these years?' she repeated in amazement as she watched the heat surge up into his face. 'Daniel, you can't mean... How many years *do* you mean?'

The answer was a long time coming and before he spoke he tried to slip away from her but she wouldn't allow it, still revelling in the startling fact that he was sharing his body with her.

'Thirty-two years,' he admitted gruffly, clearly dreading the obvious questions.

Sarian silently absorbed the fact that, until a few minutes ago, neither of them had ever made love before.

For someone of Daniel's charm and good looks, that fact was nothing short of astounding and, at some time in the near future, she hoped he would tell her why.

In the meantime, there was only one thing she wanted to know.

'Hey, Daniel,' she said softly and tilted her hips suggestively, 'tell me...was it worth waiting for?'

CHAPTER NINE

'ANNIE, are you sure you know what you're doing?' Maddie said as she followed her into the kitchen the next morning.

Sarian turned to face her but kept silent, her mind already too full of private thoughts that needed sorting through to cope with her friend's untimely interference.

What she saw made her pause a moment, the usually serene expression on Maddie's face disturbed by her obvious concern for a friend of many years.

'Annie, I'll admit Daniel's an excellent doctor and great guy, but…'

'And he's your friend and you've been pushing the two of us together almost since I moved in here with you,' Sarian finished for her with a touch of anger.

It had taken every bit of courage she possessed to take such a giant step and now Maddie, the one person she thought she could count on for support, was trying to tell her she'd made a mistake…again.

'So, Maddie, Daniel and I obliged your matchmaking efforts and got together. So why are you complaining?'

'Not like *this*, Annie,' she exclaimed. 'It's not right for you this way. Not coming in with only minutes to get yourself ready to go to work having spent the night…'

Maddie shook her head and Sarian watched her clenching her fingers in agitation and heard her draw in a sharp breath for control. 'I wanted you two to be friends because I thought his light-heartedness would be good for you. And, anyway, you were both my friends and I wanted you to like each other too.'

'We *are* friends,' Sarian said softly, knowing that was true. 'But we're also something more than friends now, and it's completely out of your control. Please, Maddie, you're my friend, and I've appreciated your help and support for years, but don't interfere.'

It felt as if her relationship with Daniel was out of *her* control too, she thought as she hurried to collect a clean set of clothes.

She'd already had a shower upstairs, nearly an hour ago, but when she'd wrapped a towel around herself to go hunting in Daniel's sitting room for yesterday's discarded uniform, she in turn had been hunted...and caught.

Her second shower had been a much more hurried affair and her hair was still quite wet.

Maddie had a cup of tea waiting for her when she emerged, and a piece of toast spread with butter and honey.

'I'm sorry, Annie,' she said quietly when she gestured towards her peace-offering. 'I know it's none of my business, but...I don't want you to get hurt. Either of you.'

'Oh, Maddie. Always the carer.' Sarian gave her a quick hug of acceptance, then sighed. 'Surely you've realised by now that caring doesn't automatically mean that you can protect people from pain?'

'But Daniel's so different from you. You're so quiet and self-contained and he's such a charmer.'

Sarian smiled almost secretively.

At first, she'd made the mistake of seeing only Daniel's public persona too. The fact that he'd hidden his deeper shadows from even Maddie's sensitive antennae had to mean that either she was more attuned to him, or that he had actually allowed her to see beneath the surface.

She had a feeling Maddie would be shocked if she knew exactly how alike her two apparently mismatched friends were.

'Well, it depends whether you believe in ''like to like'' or ''opposites attract'', Maddie. All I'm going to say is that I've never felt like this before, in all my life, and even if it lasts only hours, or days, or weeks, it will have been worth every minute.'

'But, Annie...an affair?' Maddie was clearly unhappy. 'You work with the man and you're living in the same house. What happens when it all...falls apart?'

'When, or if? We'll cope with it, the way we have to cope with anything—one step at a time and one day at a time,' Sarian said softly. 'Don't bother cooking anything for me if you're first in tonight. I don't know what my plans are yet.'

Almost as soon as hand-over was completed, Sarian found herself dealing with a patient she recognised from her first day in the department.

'Alison? What are you doing in here again so soon?' she demanded as she beckoned them through from the early morning lull of the waiting area. She joined the little family in a cubicle and pulled the curtain across.

'It's bad again, Sister,' the youngster said as Sarian helped her up onto the bed, her pale face evidence of the gastric pain she was suffering. 'I've been sick all night and I've got the runs.'

'Her temperature's high too,' added her mother. 'She

can't face eating or drinking anything and she can't bear having anything pressing over her tummy.'

'Let's get your things off and get the doctor in to look,' Sarian suggested gently.

She was sad for the youngster. Alison had presented with acute ileitis towards the end of October, and, as her inflamed intestine had responded so well to the palliative treatment with anticholinergic drugs, there had been hope that it wasn't the start of a lifetime of Crohn's disease.

Now she was back again, and, from the symptoms Sarian was seeing, in a far more acute condition this time.

'Hey, sweetheart. Couldn't wait to come back to see me, could you?' Daniel teased as he gently palpated the painful quadrant of her belly. 'I'm sorry if I'm hurting you, but I'll give you something for the pain as soon as I can.'

Sarian exchanged a glance and a reassuring smile with Alison's parents while Daniel continued his examination. She knew from their expressions that they trusted him, but they couldn't know about the deep swell of love that threatened to overtake her as she watched his gentle touch.

Once again, she found herself imagining the way he would take care of his own child; the love he would lavish on him or her and the nonsense and tall tales he would tell.

It was with a mixture of relief and disappointment that she'd done her calculations this morning and realised that the crazy chances they'd taken last night weren't going to have any lasting repercussions. Well, not in the form of babies, anyway, she thought as she watched him straighten up and stand with those sexy green eyes of his narrowed in concentration.

'This is different,' he said briefly, turning to the waiting parents. 'I know we aren't the ones going through the pain, but this episode definitely seems different to the first one.'

'Is that bad?' Alison's mother asked fearfully.

'To be honest, I don't know yet,' he admitted. 'I'm going to get a technician in to do an ultrasound scan to see if we can learn anything that way.'

'Ultrasound? But she's only eleven. She can't possibly be pregnant!' her father exclaimed, highly incensed.

'I wouldn't expect it for a minute,' Daniel said, calming him with his usual charming touch. 'Most people only hear about ultrasound in connection with pregnancy and don't realise that it has many other uses when we're trying to avoid unnecessary exploratory surgery.'

Alison gave a sudden mew of distress and was very sick again. Tears of misery started rolling down her cheeks to join the fine film of sweat and she began to sob softly when Sarian stooped to wash her face.

'I hate being sick,' she whispered dolefully. 'And it hurts my tummy.'

'So, how long will it take before she can have the test?' her mother prompted urgently. 'It can't be good for her, being like this.'

'I'm going to arrange it straight away, and I'll be back again to tell you what's happening as soon as we've got some results.'

Sarian beckoned one of the juniors across to sit with Alison, warning her about the unexpected bouts of vomiting before she left her.

She caught up with Daniel just as he put the phone down on the desk at the nurses' station.

'What do you think? Is it Crohn's disease?' she asked quietly, knowing only too well what sort of life Alison could expect to lead if the diagnosis was confirmed. Visits like this to the hospital would become part of the normal pattern of her life, as would a myriad dietary restrictions and medications.

Bouts of intestinal obstruction or intractable abscesses would mean surgery, not to mention vigilance against the increased incidence of bowel cancer in severe cases. And she was only eleven.

'Can't be sure, yet, but I've got a funny feeling about this one,' Daniel said thoughtfully. 'I've just spoken to Mark Summers, to warn them that I'm almost certain that she's going to need to come up for surgery.'

'Surgery?' Sarian was shocked. 'What do you think is going on?'

'I'll tell you as soon as I know,' he promised, beckoning her to follow him. 'In the meantime, I reckon we've got about thirty seconds before anyone notices we've gone missing.'

His wicked grin should have warned her, but the suggestive lift of one eyebrow outside the door to the sterile stores set her chuckling.

'Daniel,' she murmured, fighting down a matching grin as she leaned close enough to brush against him. 'If what you've got in mind can be completed in thirty seconds, I'm not interested.'

'But it would be a very *good* thirty seconds,' he pointed out with a hopeful expression. 'I've been practising…hard.'

'Blowing your own trumpet?' she challenged.

'I'd rather wait for you to do it,' he whispered suggestively, and when her cheeks flamed he sauntered away, chuckling.

'Rat!' she muttered to his retreating back, refusing to look at the tempting shape of that tight male bottom in case she started remembering what it had looked like with soap bubbles sliding over it in the shower. 'Just you wait till I've finished with you. You won't have enough breath to blow on your coffee, let alone blow a trumpet.'

The memory of their shared shower, some time in the middle of the night, reminded her of the heartbreaking conversation they'd had when they'd returned to the bed.

Although he'd encouraged her to reciprocate by soaping him all over, she'd carefully bitten her tongue while she'd run her hands over the numerous scars ridging the width of his back, determined not to ask questions until he was ready to volunteer the information.

They'd returned to his bed with their arms wrapped around each other and she'd been slowly drifting towards sleep when he'd begun speaking, his voice an almost inaudible whisper.

'They beat me,' he said softly, confirming her fears.

'Who?' she breathed, hardly able to imagine the misery of a child sent to an uncaring home with no one to turn to when everything went wrong. Or a poorly supervised boarding-school with unchecked bullying, or...

'My parents,' he said, robbing her of speech completely.

'But...why?' she demanded, knowing before he answered that there could *never* be a reason for beating any child, especially severely enough to leave scarring like that.

'To beat the devil out of me,' he said in a voice that sounded as if he was quoting someone else. 'Sometimes, I used to wish that the devil would just come and take me away. It seemed that hell couldn't be any worse than the place I was living.'

Sarian tightened her arms round him silently and held on. Her eyes were burning with the need to cry for the traumatised child he must have been, but the man he was now wouldn't have wanted that.

'It was a smallholding, with the accent on small,' he continued. 'They were determined to have as little to do with the sinful, evil outside world as possible, which meant working all hours to get that stony scrap of land to yield enough to support us.'

'Didn't anybody know what was going on? What about your neighbours, your teachers at school?' She was amazed that, given his beginnings, he'd ended up the well-adjusted highly qualified man he was now.

'There was no contact with the neighbours allowed, and I was eleven before the educational bureaucracy caught up with me. My father fought to a standstill to try to keep me on the farm with daily readings from the big old family Bible for my instruction. Passages chosen to reinforce his views on parental rights and duties, of course.'

'He only let you read the Bible?' Sarian was horrified, especially when she contrasted his upbringing with her own. She'd virtually been force-fed education almost from the moment she'd emerged from the womb.

'Oh, no. *He* did the reading, to make sure I didn't get any ideas above my station.'

'But…'

'He didn't realise how good my memory was, because after he'd finished the lesson of the day I'd sneak back in and find the words for myself until I worked out how to read too.'

She felt the silent huff of amusement that tightened his stomach muscles under her hand before he continued.

'The first time I brought a report card home was just a month after I'd started school. I was bottom in every lesson except religious studies and he was delighted. It looked as if he'd been right all along. It didn't stop him beating me for it, though.'

'I bet you didn't stay at the bottom for long,' she ventured with a sad smile, having learned at first hand about Daniel Burr's brand of determination.

'True. But I kept my grades secret from then on, right up until I found myself a job to earn enough to put a roof over my head because I knew he would try to stop me…try to force me to stay on the farm. Then I applied to go to a sixth-form college and, when I got the grades, later applied for a place at medical school.'

'And here you are, about to become a paediatric consultant any day now when Tim retires,' she whispered, suddenly understanding the intensity of his reaction to any form of child abuse. 'That's why you went into Paediatrics, isn't it? To help the ones who can't help themselves.'

'Don't make me out to be some sort of saint, Sarian, because I'm not,' he warned. 'I do my job to the best of my ability, and that's all I ask for in my life.'

Sarian remembered his words with a shiver.

They'd been as clear a declaration as he could make

without spelling it out in words of one syllable. Daniel wasn't interested in a long-term commitment, and, with his history, who could blame him?

Mind you, she thought with a brief spark of hope, he'd never taken anyone else to his bed, so that was proof of some sort that he'd changed since he'd met her. Perhaps, in time, he would realise that he could love her the way she'd fallen in love with him.

In the meantime, her own life had been turned on its head by a man she found so attractive in both spirit and appearance that, not only was she unable to resist him, but she didn't *want* to resist him.

'Come with me, Sarian,' Daniel said suddenly, breaking into her introspection. 'I've got some news for Alison and her family, and as you've got to know them...'

She hurried along in his wake, having to take extra steps every so often to keep up with his much longer stride, but she was determined to be in on this meeting.

'I've got some bad news and some good news,' he announced when he joined the little family in the cubicle.

'If I've got a choice, I'll have the bad news first,' Alison's mother said hurriedly. 'At least, then, I know there's good news to follow.'

'Well, the bad news is that, in a couple of minutes, Alison's going to be on her way up to theatre for an operation.' He raised a hand to stifle the poor woman's gasp. 'And the good news is that this time, all she's got is common or garden appendicitis.'

'It's *not* CD this time?' her husband demanded in disbelief. 'But it came on just like that other episode.'

'That's right. The two conditions can have very similar beginnings, but this time Alison's struck the jack-pot and got the one we can cure permanently.'

Neither of the parents seemed to know whether to laugh or cry and Sarian felt decidedly misty-eyed by the time she saw Mick Monaghan wheeling them on their way to the lifts and thence to theatre.

'Don't take this the wrong way, but I do hope I never see Alison again,' Sarian said fervently.

'Well, there's no evidence of any other members of her family suffering with Crohn's, or ulcerative colitis, so that's a good start,' Daniel pointed out. 'If she's careful with her diet—'

'And lucky,' Sarian added, knowing how much such an intangible element could play a part.

Their paths diverged for a while, with Sarian taking charge of triage while Maddie and Daniel spent nearly an hour in and out of one of the treatment rooms trying to stabilise a young asthmatic patient.

By the time Sarian was relieved to go for her break, she was looking forward to catching a glimpse of Daniel. Perhaps he was suffering from withdrawal symptoms, too, and would be free to join her?

The weather outside was grim and, after their activities last night, she was already exhausted when it was only halfway through her shift.

Even so, she had a smile on her face and an extra spring in her step as she made her way towards the treatment room where she expected to find their asthmatic patient being readied for a stay up on the ward.

She could hear the sound of voices but couldn't make out what they were saying until she was almost outside the treatment-room doors.

'Daniel, have you thought about what you're doing? Do you realise how easy it would be to hurt her?' That was Maddie in her 'mother-hen' mode, again, Sarian recognised with a brief grimace.

'Look, Maddie, you wouldn't tell me a thing about her problems when she arrived; just told me to find out for myself—if she'd tell me. So, *you* know I only set out to find out why she kept the world at a distance. You can hardly blame me if I've given her a bit of self-confidence along the way.'

Sarian's smile dimmed.

Was that how he saw the pleasure they'd given each other last night—as a way of boosting her self-confidence? It had certainly been much more than that for her.

'I admit she's different, today,' Maddie said grudgingly. 'I could almost feel jealous of the way her feet hardly touch the floor. I daren't ask what you've done to my quiet, serious friend Annie.'

'What can I say?' Daniel said jokingly, his voice suddenly drawing nearer. 'It's my devastating charm that does it, every time.'

Before Sarian could move away the treatment-room door swung open leaving her facing Daniel from a distance of just a few feet.

'Ah...there you are,' she stammered. 'I—I'm just going for my break and I was looking for you to see if you were due...'

'Good idea,' he said with a wide smile that seemed devoid of any subterfuge. 'I'll just check to see if there's anything else that needs doing before I disappear.'

He strode off towards the nurses' station leaving Sarian facing Maddie.

'Annie,' Maddie began with a slightly guilty look.

'I don't know what you heard, but I promise I was only—'

'Don't,' Sarian said sharply. 'I told you politely this morning not to interfere. Now I'm saying it bluntly. Stay out of it, Maddie. You're not my mother. It's *my* life, good, bad or indifferent, so let me live it.'

She was shaking as she turned on her heel and walked away from Maddie, the image of the stricken look on her friend's face making her feel slightly sick.

Then she saw Daniel waiting for her, his familiar stance of folded arms and crossed ankles while he leaned one shoulder against the nearest convenient wall setting her heart thumping to a different rhythm.

She drew closer and saw that smile on his face again—the one she'd seen when he'd opened the treatment-room door and seen her standing there.

He unfolded his arms and held his hand out to her and, like a flash of light in a darkened room, she realised that for the first time in her life she was learning what it was like to have a man openly glad to see her.

It actually made her feel…confident…beautiful…

'So, when are you going to talk to me?' Daniel prompted with a teasing smile.

They'd found an empty table tucked right at the back of the room and were sitting side by side to eat their meal, like a couple of adolescents.

In spite of their ages, that was more or less what they were, Sarian realised when she thought of how little experience either of them had acquired with the opposite sex—until last night.

And if tonight was anything like the previous one, they would soon be catching up on their contemporaries…

'Sarian?' Daniel nudged her and she realised she'd been so busy imagining the delights to come that she'd completely forgotten to enjoy the present moment.

'Sorry. I was wool-gathering.' She smiled up into clear green eyes and felt her heart turn over inside her chest when she couldn't see a sign of the shadows that used to live there. 'What did you say?'

'I asked when you were going to talk to me,' he repeated patiently. 'I've spilled my guts to you over the last twenty-four hours or so, and you've stayed as close-mouthed as ever.'

'It's not really important any more,' Sarian said, and realised that it was true.

All the old heartaches that she'd been carrying around with her for years; all the misery that had weighed her down like so much unnecessary baggage; all of it seemed to have fallen away from her shoulders, leaving her feeling as if she were light enough to fly.

If only she hadn't had those cross words with Maddie, everything would be right with her world.

'But...'

A colourful poster caught her eye and she recognised in an instant that it was publicising the Christmas Ball, due to take place shortly before the festive holidays.

'Oh, Daniel, I can't tell you how different I feel about...about everything,' she finished expansively.

She gestured towards the poster.

'Take that, for instance. A month ago, I would have known that Maddie was going to find some way to twist my arm to go to it and I would have been spending half my time trying to find ways to get out of it.'

'You did the same with the Halloween disco and I never did find out why,' he said pointedly. 'Obviously,

I had some theories, but since last night most of them have gone by the board...'

'Such as?' Suddenly she was intrigued to know what he'd been thinking.

For a moment she thought he was going to explain, but a group of chattering junior nurses descended on the table beside them and their cocoon of privacy disappeared.

'Look, when do you finish tonight?' he demanded with a quick glance at his watch.'

'I'm on a long day, today.' She pulled a face. 'I started at seven-thirty this morning and I'll finish at eight tonight.'

She held her breath, hoping he was going to suggest she waited for him in his flat. She could easily use the key he'd given to Maddie; the key she'd used when she'd gone upstairs to confront him and had surprised him emerging from his bathroom...

The silence seemed to drag out interminably and she hurried into speech to hide her disappointment.

'Actually, I need to do a load of laundry as soon as I get back or I'm going to run out of clean uniforms. I'll probably hear you when you get home.'

Home, she thought as they made their way back to the department. For some strange reason, the converted Victorian house just a few streets away from Lizzie's felt more like home than any other place she'd stayed—including the house in which she'd lived with her parents.

They'd just entered the A and E department, and she'd made up her mind to offer to make him a meal ready for his homecoming, when they were buttonholed by the consultant.

'Daniel. Good lad, you're here,' Tim Robertson said genially. 'Come and have a look at this.'

Before Sarian had time to say a word they were striding off together back towards the X-ray department.

Sarian had one load in the washing machine and the other nearly finished in the tumble-drier when she heard the thump of the front door and a set of footsteps making for the stairs.

Daniel was home!

Her heart executed a quick barrel-roll inside her chest and her pulse took off for the stratosphere.

She glanced round at the machines. They were both doing what they were supposed to do and there was absolutely no reason why she shouldn't leave them to get on with it while she went up to say hello to Daniel.

Perhaps he would be ready to listen to her offer of a meal now. It wouldn't take long to make a quick omelette, or even a stir-fry.

She set off up the stairs, half convinced that she had wings on her feet rather than lightweight trainers as she hurried towards Daniel's flat.

She could feel the smile creeping over her face as she anticipated the welcome waiting for her.

Would he take her in his arms and kiss her as soon as she set foot in his flat? Would their kisses become too urgent for him to want to wait for her to cook a meal? She was beginning to wonder whether it was even worth offering.

She'd reached the bottom of the final flight before she realised that she could hear him talking, the disjointed speech telling her that it was half of a telephone conversation.

She slowed down to give him some privacy then realised that his voice was unusually clear because he'd left his door ajar.

Had he done that deliberately, as a silent invitation for her to walk straight in, or had it been an oversight when he'd hurried in to answer the phone?

'No, Rob, I promise you, it won't be causing a problem,' Daniel said, keen to put his friend's mind at rest. 'I said you were welcome to share the flat, and I meant it.'

He pulled a face at the abysmal timing.

Here was Rob wanting to come down almost immediately so he could start looking for a place of his own, and all Daniel could think about was what it would do to his new relationship with Sarian.

He'd actually forgotten that he'd made that offer, and had spent his journey home from Lizzie's imagining her response when he invited her to spend her nights with him. Perhaps she would even agree to move in with him...

'I'm glad you're coming to Lizzie's, too,' he said. 'You're joining a good staff and I think you'll fit in well. I also happen to think we've got the prettiest nurses in the hospital, but then I'm biased. Maddie and Sarian actually live in the same house so you'll meet them first.'

'You seem different, Easy,' Rob said with a rusty chuckle, and Daniel noticed that he'd ignored his hint about the female population in the department. 'Is it Maddie or Sarian that's caused the changes? Don't tell me you're finally starting to think about marriage and commitment?'

'Marriage and commitment?' Daniel scoffed in an

automatic reflex honed over many years. 'They're the last thing I'm looking for. The next Ice Age will arrive before that happens.'

He didn't have time to ponder the strange hollowness in the oft-repeated words because an unexpected sound, like that of a sharply drawn breath, had him whirling towards the door...the partly open door...

He strained his ears, hoping he'd been wrong, but the sudden sound of retreating footsteps left him feeling sick.

There was an ache in his chest as if his heart had just been carved out with a blunt cleaver, and it only grew worse each time he replayed the words she must have heard.

He could only imagine the way her wide grey eyes would have darkened with hurt.

'Easy? Hey, Dan, are you still there?'

Distracted, he brought the conversation to a rapid close, his mind full of only one thought.

He must find Sarian. He must get her to listen while he explained...

While he explained what, exactly?

CHAPTER TEN

SARIAN did her crying in the laundry room.

With the lights turned out so that no one would think of looking for her there, she'd sobbed her heart out under the high-pitched cover of spinning machinery.

By the time both loads were finished and folded, she'd washed her face and regained her composure and was ready to face Maddie.

'Daniel was looking for you,' Maddie said without even looking away from the programme on the screen.

'I've been upstairs. He was on the phone,' Sarian replied briefly, carefully neglecting to say that her visit had been earlier than his had, and the cause of it.

She was glad that her friend was watching television when she let herself into the flat—at least the lights were dim enough to hide the residual puffiness around her eyes. By the morning, there would be nothing left to show for her disastrous descent into the world of the one-night stand. Her one and only spectacular fling.

She firmly shut the thought away and carried on through to the bathroom. By the time she finished in there, Maddie should be ready to let her have her temporary bedroom to herself.

She was on late shift tomorrow. With more than twelve hours for her grandmother's good Welsh grit to bolster her up, she'd be ready to face Daniel.

Anyway, her job was one that provided plenty to do to occupy both her mind and her hands, because patient care could never be dependent on the whims of a nurse's love life—or lack of it.

Her final thought as she punched her pillow into a comfortable shape was the one that had been a recurrent theme in her life.

'I'm a survivor,' she whispered fiercely. 'No matter what happens, I *am* a survivor.'

When she finally fell asleep she must have slept very soundly because she didn't even hear Maddie getting up for work the next morning.

The first thing she heard was the sound of a key in the lock and for one dreadful moment she thought she'd slept the whole day away and that this was Maddie returning home.

No such luck, she thought when Daniel strode in as if he owned the place and stood at the end of her makeshift bed.

'Where did you disappear to last night?' he demanded bluntly, his brows drawn down over eyes that were almost shooting sparks at her.

'What do you care?' she shot back, determined not to feel at a disadvantage in spite of the fact she was still in her bed.

She calmly reached for her dressing gown, draped over the arm of the settee at her head, and wrapped it around her to cover the oversized T-shirt she wore as a nightdress.

While she'd waited for sleep to come, she'd replayed all the little clues that should have warned her what had been going to happen.

The fact that he'd been at such pains to seek out her company had fooled her until she'd mentally replayed his conversation with Maddie. She should have known that her friend would have enlisted his help to 'bring her out of her shell'.

Unfortunately, her grandmother's saying, 'There's none so blind as those that *will* not see,' was only too true. She'd deliberately closed her eyes to the fact that someone like Daniel would never be interested in someone as ordinary as her. It had taken his conversation with Rob to clear her vision.

She would just have to get used to the fact that he felt free to walk into the flat unannounced. It wasn't because he couldn't wait to see her. In spite of the masterful performance he'd put on the night before last, she knew he was never going to be overcome with lust at the sight of her. *That* message had been well and truly rammed home.

Holding his gaze with a glare of her own, she slid her feet to the ground.

'What do you mean? Of course I care,' he retorted, raking impatient fingers through his hair. 'I thought you were going to be coming up to eat with me last night.'

One strand of hair escaped to curve over his forehead and in spite of herself her fingers itched to smooth it back for him.

'I did, but you were otherwise engaged at the time,' she said coldly. 'I didn't intend eavesdropping, but at least it let me know where I stood before I made a real fool of myself. Now, if you don't mind, I want to get up and I'd like you out of here.'

'Sarian, don't be stupid,' he began, taking a step towards her.

A tiny corner of her mind registered the way he said her name and was willing to soften when it registered the appearance of pain in his eyes again. The rest of her knew only too well where such softness led and hardened her heart against succumbing.

'That was yesterday, Daniel,' she said sharply, stopping him in his tracks. 'Yesterday and the day before I was stupid, letting myself believe in the possibility of love and happily ever after. Today, I know better, thanks to your unwitting honesty. When he arrives in the department, I shall have to convey my gratitude to Robert for his part in bringing me to my senses.'

'Dammit, Sarian, that conversation was a casual one between two friends and wasn't meant to be heard out of context. It wasn't what it sounded like.' He took another step towards her, close enough for her to see that his eyes had darkened to deep green, the way they'd been when he'd taken her in his arms and...

Enough, she told herself. Forget all that and deal with today.

'So, you're telling me that the night we spent together was special?'

'Of course it was. How could you think otherwise?' That hurt was in his voice now.

'Does that mean you've changed your mind? That it won't take until the next Ice Age before you start thinking about marriage and commitment?'

She took a mean pleasure in seeing him wince as she threw his own words back at him.

'I told you, that wasn't what it sounded like,' he repeated, obviously unhappy. 'That phrase is just one that Rob and I have been throwing backwards and forwards almost since we first met at medical school.'

'So, does that mean that the night before last was the start of a long-term commitment between us, eventually leading to marriage?'

Her deliberately challenging words seemed to hang in the air between them and she saw his face grow still.

Over the last couple of minutes he must have thought she was swallowing his explanation because she'd watched the tension gradually leaving his body. It was back with a vengeance now.

'Well, not exactly,' he said uncomfortably. 'After all, we haven't known each other very long and it would be stupid to go rushing headlong into any-thing…' He shrugged helplessly when he ran out of words.

'Anything permanent?' she finished for him, know-ing as well as he did that it was the word he'd been going to use…or, rather, the word he'd been trying to avoid using. Where was the glib charm when he needed it? she thought unkindly.

Oh, he still had the beautiful face of a fallen angel and eyes that made her heart turn over, but if he didn't feel any of the overwhelming love she'd begun to feel for him then the only thing she could do was cut her losses. She'd honestly believed that she could cope with some sort of affair with him, but once she'd real-ised how much she'd come to love him…

'Don't look so worried, Daniel,' she said sweetly. 'I should be thanking you for you efforts over the last couple of weeks in drawing me out of my shell. Now I can try my hand and see if my grandmother was right when she said there were plenty more fish in the sea.'

She knew she wasn't going to find a better exit line, not in the few seconds she had left before her careful façade crumbled.

With one last fake smile in his direction she grabbed her wash bag and escaped into the bathroom.

She thought of waiting to run the tap so that she

could be sure he left the flat, but almost as soon as she threw the bolt on the door she heard the slam confirming his departure.

Strangely, that unexpected display of temper on Daniel's part dispelled her threatening tears and stiffened her backbone.

By the time she arrived at Lizzie's she was back on an even keel and ready for anything.

Standing under her shower she'd remembered another saying she'd heard—not one of her grandmother's this time. 'If life gives you lemons, make lemonade,' she repeated to herself. Her affair with Daniel might be one of the shortest events in romantic history, but it had certainly left her with enough memories to last for years.

Now she had work to do, and Daniel *Easy* Burr wasn't going to mess that up.

In the event, she found it all too easy to switch off from her disappointment with a steady stream of sick and injured children to deal with.

She had hardly hung her jacket up when an ambulance came flying up to the emergency entrance with a youngster who had been trapped when a pile of bricks had fallen on him.

The fact that he'd been trespassing on a building site when he should have been at school was unimportant when they were trying to establish whether he was just badly bruised or had sustained head or spinal injuries at the same time as his multiple cuts and grazes.

It took three of them to persuade him to stay still while he was systematically examined from head to foot, and a threat of loss of television privileges from his worried mother if he didn't comply while they took X-rays.

It was a relief all round when no breaks were found, but their patient wasn't happy when he was told he was being sent up to a ward for several hours of observation before he could be released.

'Well, I'm grateful he was OK, even if *he* wasn't,' Jenny Barber muttered. 'I see him and wonder if it's what my little monsters are going to be like in a few years.'

Sarian laughed but it sounded rather hollow to her ears. For all her worries, at least Jenny had a loving, supportive husband and two gorgeous, healthy children to go home to at the end of her shift.

Enough, she reminded herself. You've gone all these years without thinking about what you were missing, so it shouldn't be too hard to shut down again—not for a determined woman.

Her next patient was rushed in almost on the heels of the last, a little girl with blood-spattered dressings all over her face and arms.

'This is Megan. She's three and she's been attacked by a neighbour's dog,' the paramedic reported quickly. 'Multiple lacerations and abrasions to face, neck, hands and arms. Ear partially severed. We got two IVs up and running and she's been on Entonox all the way in.'

'See if you can get hold of Gareth Davies up on Plastics,' Daniel said before he bent forward to introduce himself to the shivering child. 'Hello, sweet pea, my name's Daniel. I'm a doctor and I'm going to help take the hurt away. OK?'

The little blonde moppet nodded jerkily and earned herself one of his special smiles.

Sarian swallowed. How typical of Daniel to stick to the essentials, knowing that was all the child needed to hear.

Around him, the team was going through the routine, connecting her to the continuous monitoring equipment, taking blood samples for cross-matching, removing her torn, blood-stained clothing, but Daniel didn't falter in his steady stream of chatter.

One by one he lifted the increasingly blood-soaked dressings and assessed the degree of damage. Working beside him, Sarian saw the myriad puncture wounds where the dog's teeth had bitten down on her tender flesh and she couldn't help wincing when she saw the way her skin had ripped almost like wet tissue paper.

Gareth Davies was going to have his work cut out if he was going to be able to put this jigsaw back together without her looking like an extra from a low-budget horror film.

'Poor little scrap,' she muttered as she watched little Megan on her way out of the department. 'For all his skill, Gareth is never going to be able to return her to the way she was before this happened.'

'Even if she were to get millions in compensation from the owner of the dog, it can't turn the clock back,' Lisa Chan agreed as she brushed sympathetic tears from her cheeks. 'She must have looked like a little fairy doll before this happened.'

Sarian gave her shoulder a squeeze as she went past, knowing that Lisa's soft heart often had her in tears.

Sometimes days were like that, she mused a little later. Just one thing after another wrenching at your heart. Like the child who'd just been rushed through with all the classic signs of meningitis, right down to the distinctive rash that was evidence of generalised septicaemia.

Her parents were absolutely distraught. She'd only had a snuffly cold when they'd put her down for her nap, and within hours it looked as if she was close to dying.

The large noisy man barging through the entrance doors not two minutes later was a different matter entirely.

For a start, he'd obviously been drinking, for all that he was wearing a city gent's suit and an expensive silk tie.

It was the way he was carrying the child that had Sarian darting forward, as if it were of no more importance than a rag doll although he must have been about two years old.

'He fell and hit his head,' the man announced loudly. 'I thought I ought to let you have a look at him when he wouldn't wake up.'

'When did he hit it?' Sarian demanded, her eyes immediately spotting the large bruise on the side of the baby's head, very close to his temple. 'And what did he hit it on?'

'About half an hour ago, give or take,' he replied vaguely without answering the second question at all.

Sarian had whisked the little child through to the resuscitation room, knowing that one of the receptionists had seen what was happening and was notifying staff at the nurses' station.

She'd placed him gently on the bed and checked that he was still breathing before she slipped an oxygen mask in position, then started stripping his clothing away.

'Hey! What're you doing that for?' the man demanded, his hand clamping on her elbow hard. 'He's only hit his head.'

'I still have to check him over to make sure he doesn't have any other injuries from the fall,' she said firmly, tugging her arm out of his grasp and beginning again.

'I said, I only brought him in here for you to look at his head,' the man said insistently, his voice growing louder with each word as he grabbed her shoulder and swung her round to face him.

Sarian couldn't help grimacing at the smell of sour whisky on his breath. From a distance of only a few inches it was quite nauseating.

'I'm sorry, sir, but I have to do my job,' she said resolutely as she twisted away and leaned over the child again. 'Perhaps you'd like to go and wait outside while I finish?'

'Listen, bitch, I know what your game is,' he shouted as he wrenched her away from the defenceless baby and flung her against the wall. 'I'm a respectable man around here. You're not going to get a chance of making out that I injured the kid just because he's got a few bruises.'

He'd followed her on her stumbling path backwards across the room and before she could regain her balance had his hands around her throat and pinned her against the wall.

'So what if he's got a few bruises? Kids are always falling over,' he blustered, his hands tightening inexorably. 'It's you self-righteous cows that really get to me. What do you know? You don't have to put up with a kid whingeing by the hour; you just send them home. How can anyone concentrate when the bloody kid won't keep quiet? You tell me that. Eh?'

But Sarian was beyond telling him anything, her fight for breath waning as everything began to go black.

'Let her go!' roared a blessedly familiar voice. 'Take

your hands off her, you bastard, and let her go! Security! Here! Now!'

Suddenly the pressure on her windpipe was gone and she gasped desperately for a lungful of precious air even as she crumpled towards the floor.

'Easy. Nice and easy,' the voice crooned and she knew without opening her eyes that it was Daniel who had caught her and was lifting her into his arms. 'Come on, my love, open your eyes.'

An hour later Sarian was sitting in the back of a taxi on her way back to the flat with Daniel's arm wrapped firmly around her.

She still couldn't believe the speed with which her attacker had been subdued by Head of Security, Jock MacGregor, watching from her position on the other bed in the room as Daniel had focused his attention on the little lad lying in front of him.

Once his clothes had been removed, she'd caught enough glimpses to see that his little body had been almost covered with bruises. Just thinking about it made her shudder.

'Easy,' Daniel whispered. 'It's all over now.'

'Not for little James,' she whispered, her throat still too painful for normal speech.

Daniel swore under his breath. 'I've seen dogs treated better than some people treat their children,' he muttered as the taxi drew up outside the house.

Sarian got out and hunted for her keys, expecting Daniel to turn around and go back to Lizzie's.

'I'll do that,' he said and ushered her into the welcome warmth of the building.

'But...' She was grateful for his presence...very grateful...but he was supposed to be on duty.

'Lizzie's takes care of its own,' he said, answering the unspoken question. 'I've taken time off to look after you.'

The tenderness in his expression and his voice was almost too much for her to bear and she was concentrating so hard on fighting her tears that she barely noticed that he was taking her up to his flat instead of her own.

'Daniel, I just…I need to get out of these clothes. I need to get clean. I just feel so…so *contaminated*…'

'Shh, my love. It's all organised,' he said soothingly and led her through to his bathroom to turn on the taps and adjust the temperature.

She was too grateful for his help to feel embarrassed, her hands shaking uncontrollably as the shock began to grip her.

'Easy, my love, easy,' he crooned as he joined her under the warm water, his clothes instantly saturated as he held her tightly in his arms.

The first sob was wrenched out of her in spite of her best efforts and then the dam burst.

It took a long time for the tears to abate, but slowly she became aware that Daniel's soothing murmurs weren't just random sounds but real words of admiration and praise.

She drew in a shuddering breath and lifted her head off his shoulder.

'Daniel? Why have you got your clothes on in the shower?'

'Because you needed someone to hold you,' he said simply.

'But, shouldn't you have taken them off first?' Her brain didn't seem to be working very fast.

'Not if I wanted to stay sane,' he said, his voice a

low growl. 'Dammit, Sarian, there's no way I could stand naked with you in this shower.'

'You did before,' she pointed out, looking away from his knowing eyes when she remembered what had happened next.

Gently, he tilted her chin up till she met his gaze again.

'Exactly,' he said, his eyes dark and hot. 'And that was *before* I realised I was in love with you.'

'You're...?' The words caught in her throat and she shook her head. 'But, Daniel, you said...'

'Shh.' He put one finger over her lips to still the words. 'I know what I said, and I knew as soon as I said it that it wasn't true. I'm going to have to learn to mince my words—it'll make them easier to swallow.'

'But...love?' She couldn't help staring up at him, even though she knew her own heart would be in her eyes.

'Yes. *Love*,' he said firmly. 'And if it took watching you having the life squeezed out of you to bring it home to me, then all I can do is apologise for being slow. My excuse is my lack of practice in recognising it.'

'How much practice do you need?' There was a deep warmth spreading through her, banishing all the cold dark places she'd lived with so long.

'Less than a second if I look into your eyes, assuming that it's love I'm seeing there?'

There was an endearing hint of uncertainty in his eyes and his voice that she was able to dispel with a fervent 'Yes!' and a kiss.

'On the other hand,' he mused, leaning forward to turn off the taps and reach for a towel, 'if we take it nice and easy, we could still be reassuring each other in about fifty years' time?'

'We're late, again,' Sarian pointed out as she carefully negotiated the marble steps leading to the hotel ball-room.

'And we're not staying long,' Daniel reminded her. 'You promised.'

She could already hear the music and the sound of several hundred members of St Elizabeth's off-duty staff enjoying themselves at the annual Christmas Ball.

'That's your fault,' Daniel said, wrapping his arm around her and pulling her close enough to nuzzle the bare expanse of her slender neck. 'You mentioned the fateful words and you had to suffer the consequences.'

'Suffer?' She raised a quizzical eyebrow. 'Ah, so that's what I was doing.' She chuckled wickedly.

Daniel's grin was equally wicked. 'To think you were such a nice girl when I met you,' he said mus-ingly, his encircling arm bringing his hand dangerously close to sensitive territory.

Sarian felt her body react to the promise in his touch and in his eyes. 'Where you're concerned, I seem to have become easy,' she whispered and slid her own hand down for a retaliatory pat, her action only hidden by the back of his jacket.

Her words reminded her of something.

'Hey, how come you never told me why your nick-name was Easy?' she demanded. 'All this time, I've been thinking that Rob knew deep dark secrets about you.'

'He did, but only the truth about my name.' He gri-maced. 'How many people do you know called Ezekiel?'

She was still laughing as they entered the room and started looking for Maddie and Rob.

With a woman's eye for colour, Sarian quickly spotted the rich forest-green of Maddie's dress and they began to cross the floor in her direction.

'She doesn't look as if she minds Rob as a partner instead of you,' Sarian pointed out as their two friends stood talking, Maddie's face more animated than she'd seen it in weeks. 'Do you think there could be something brewing between the two of them?'

'Don't even think of interfering,' Daniel warned. 'You just concentrate on us and leave them to sort themselves out.'

Sarian subsided, but resolved to keep her eyes open for further developments. She would love her friend to be as happy as she was, and as for Rob...

'Annie!' Maddie still hadn't got used to using her real name, but, from her, it didn't matter.

'Hey, Easy, I wasn't expecting to see you here. Changed your mind?' There was a teasing grin on Rob's face as he challenged Daniel.

'Not at all.' Daniel patted his pocket where the keys resided. 'Sarian just wanted us to stick our heads in the door, as it's a fund-raiser, and she wanted to tell you the result of that meeting we went to today.'

'What was it all about, Annie?' Maddie asked, suddenly serious. She knew that Sarian had been shocked to receive a letter from her parents' solicitors so long after their deaths. Apparently previous missives had never been forwarded to her new address near Lizzie's.

'Their will,' she said with a catch in her voice. 'Apparently they changed it after I went to visit them that last time, and Mum had written a letter that never got posted...'

She remembered that visit all too clearly. She'd hoped that after all the bad blood between them, they could finally begin to build a few bridges, but within days they'd gone, victims of a tragic and unnecessary accident.

'A letter?' Maddie moved a little closer, as though she'd forgotten that Sarian had Daniel's support now.

'Apparently she wrote it not long after I left, saying she was sorry they hadn't been more welcoming, but that seeing me had been a real shock. I'd changed so much they hardly recognised me at first.'

She gave a self-deprecating look down at the slender creamy dress she was wearing today. 'Hardly surprising, when I used to weigh about twice as much...' She bit her lips for control.

'What happened about the will?' Maddie prompted.

'They'd directed that everything should be disposed of except personal mementoes such as jewellery, and the proceeds were to be handed to me to dispose of in any way I saw fit.'

'And?' Maddie prompted again.

'And there's plenty for buying a house and to make some special purchases—such as those computers Lizzie's wanted to buy for the patients, and several monitors for babies at risk of SIDS.'

'There'll even be enough to buy a better brand of coffee for the staff room,' Daniel teased, 'and some packets of chocolate biscuits.'

'So, this really is the end of an era,' Maddie mused, a slightly melancholy expression on her face. 'After your wedding today...'

'Shh!' warned Daniel, but it was too late. Someone had overheard and, in spite of the noise filling the room, the words were picked up and spread like wild-fire.

In a matter of minutes Sarian and Daniel found themselves herded to the front of the ballroom as the band played a fanfare.

Someone had grabbed Daniel's retiring boss, Tim Robertson, and given him a quick résumé of the day's news, and now he stood with the two of them, a glass of something pale and sparkly in his hand.

'For those of you who haven't heard yet, our thoroughly nice Sister Williams has just thrown herself away on devilish Dr Burr.' There was a cheer mixed with a ripple of laughter when people reminded each other of Daniel's costume at the Halloween disco.

'Seriously, though,' he continued, his slightly portly face rather pink as a result of his unexpected Master of Ceremonies duties, 'I couldn't be more delighted for the two of them and that my last duty should be to wish them many happy years.'

He raised his glass, silently inviting the rest of the room to follow his lead. 'To Daniel and Sarian.'

'To Rob and Maddie,' Daniel proposed, raising a glass of the complimentary champagne they'd found waiting for them when they'd finally reached the hotel room.

They'd arrived here much later than they'd intended, finding it hard to leave when there had been so many people at the ball wanting to wish them well.

'I hope Rob and Maddie realise how much this little gesture is going to cost them,' Daniel mused as he gazed round at their ridiculously opulent surroundings.

'Don't think about it. They said they wanted to make sure we had a bit of time to ourselves, so they arranged tonight as a mini-honeymoon.'

'Uh-oh!' Daniel reached across with a wicked grin and took her glass out of her hand, only to deposit it on the ornate bedside cabinet. 'You said that word again! Are you prepared to pay the penalty?'

'Always,' she said with a chuckle, reaching up to wind her arms around his neck. 'Especially when you start off nice and easy...with a kiss...'

HARLEQUIN®
INTRIGUE

WE'LL LEAVE YOU BREATHLESS!

If you've been looking for thrilling tales of
contemporary passion and sensuous love stories
with taut, edge-of-the-seat suspense—then
you'll love Harlequin Intrigue!

Every month, you'll meet four new heroes
who are guaranteed to make your spine tingle
and your pulse pound. With them you'll enter
into the exciting world of Harlequin Intrigue—
where your life is on the line
and so is your heart!

THAT'S INTRIGUE—
ROMANTIC SUSPENSE
AT ITS BEST!

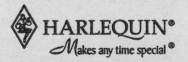

HARLEQUIN®
Makes any time special ®

Harlequin Romance ®

Delightful
Affectionate
Romantic
Emotional

Tender
Original

Daring
Riveting
Enchanting
Adventurous
Moving

Harlequin Romance ®—
capturing the world you dream of...

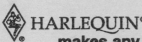